LORD CHAMBERS

C.N. CRAWFORD

SUMMARY OF CITY OF THORNS

In case you forgot, a refresher...

In book one, Rowan was determined to break into the City of Thorns.

She knew that her mother had been murdered by a demon, but she couldn't remember anything about the killer. All she had was a faint memory of a five-pointed star on the killer's forehead, and the knowledge that her mother had burned to death. The trauma from that night left her with a deep fear of fire, and an inability to remember the exact events.

One night, while out for her birthday with her best friend Shai, a powerful demon showed up at the bar. The gorgeous, silver-haired Lord of Chaos seemed to think she was his worst enemy—a succubus named Mortana. Long ago, Mortana was responsible for killing all the other Lilu (incubi and succubi). She was the reason that Orion was imprisoned for centuries. He blames Mortana for killing his family. Suffice it to say, he really loathes her—and Rowan looks exactly like her.

The next thing she knew, Rowan was in a dungeon in the demons' City of Thorns, about to be executed. Only when Orion bit her neck and tasted her mortal blood did he believe she was mortal.

Then, the two struck a deal. She would pretend to be Mortana—the succubus—and help Orion learn how to kill the king (Cambriel). Rowan would get to stay in the city, secretly hunting for her mom's killer.

The two of them work on disguising Rowan as a succubus, and as they spend more time with each other, their attraction grows. Together, they explore the city. Rowan searched for a five-pointed star, and anyone who might wield fire magic.

In the old Lilu quarter of the city, Rowan discovered a portrait of her mother hanging in an abandoned mansion. She learned that her mother had once lived as a demon aristocrat in the city, and that her father had probably burned to death outside the mansion. When the Lilu were massacred by Mortana and the king centuries ago, her parents had gone into hiding.

At last, the truth came out and shocked both of them. A shimmering key tattoo showed up on Rowan's arm, and she discovered that her magical powers had been locked as a way to hide her identity.

Rowan is not mortal, but is a succubus with fire power. Even more horrifying to Rowan is the realization that she and Orion both have the five-pointed star on their heads. Both of them have fire magic, like her mother's killer. The star she'd been searching for is a mark of Lucifer, signifying that someone is destined to rule. Rowan can't remember much from the night her mother died, but she wonders if she saw the star on her own forehead in a reflection.

As soon as Orion sees the mark on her forehead, he is convinced that she has been lying to him. Now, he is positive that she is Mortana. The two of them fight, trying to kill each other, but neither of them can bring themselves to do it.

At the end of book one, Rowan is hiding from Orion. She still does not know who killed her mother, but she has a clue in an old nursery rhyme she found in her parents' house.

CHAPTER 1—ROWAN

I gripped a plastic bag to my chest, trying to keep it dry. A slate-gray sky spread out overhead. As I stepped in a cold puddle, rain drenched my socks through the hole in my shoe.

This was my life now—kicked out of the City of Thorns, back in my old neighborhood. As soon as Orion had discovered the mark of Lucifer glowing on my head, he'd decided I was his worst enemy. The oath he'd sworn kept me out of the demon city where I belonged. If he saw me again, he'd be compelled to kill me.

Shivering, I glanced across the street at the powder-blue house where I'd grown up and the crooked statues of the Virgin Mary the owner kept on the little patch of grass out front.

Behind it, the dark Osborne Woods Reservation stretched for thousands of acres. For a moment, a memory flashed in my mind—sprinting through those woods years ago in rain like this. I shuddered, sliding my hand in my pockets to run my fingers over my keys.

Not far ahead, a woman with a stroller hurried down the sidewalk with her baby to get out of the rain. My throat tightened. Mom used to send me out for Dunkin' Donuts across the street on weekend mornings. God, I missed her. Being in this neighborhood wasn't helping.

Witchcraft Point *sounded* like a magical neighborhood of curiosity shops and cobblestones. In reality, it was the old industrial part of town, a cluster of half-abandoned, boarded-up tanneries, broken windows, and shabby rentals. Fast food joints completed the bleak suburban sprawl.

I turned to look behind me at the demon city— towering walls of golden stone and gleaming turrets on Osborne's tallest hill to the east. It was warmer inside the gates, where the amber walls glowed with an unearthly light like an ancient Mediterranean paradise. Beyond the gates, the Acheron River sprang from the ground and flowed out to the candy-blue sea.

I had to get back in there somehow. Not only was it much nicer there, but I hadn't found the person who'd burned Mom to death in Osborne Woods.

Yet.

I turned away from the city again.

After a few days outside the City of Thorns, I could feel my magic and strength seeping out of my body. It was a deeply uncomfortable feeling, like growing sicker.

I glanced to my left. On a craggy hill behind the Dunkin' parking lot, the Osborne Gallows had once stood. Hard to imagine now, but bodies had once swung on the slope behind the dumpster.

I pulled the plastic bag of sweatpants closer, hoping they wouldn't be wet by the time I arrived at the home of Mr. Esposito, my mom's nonagenarian friend. Earlier today, I'd peered out my dingy basement windows and seen him walking to the bus stop in the pouring rain. His pants had sagged to his knees on his skinny frame, and he'd shuffled along, trying to get to a bench so he could pull them up.

I'd stood at the window, frozen in indecision. Should I run out to help him, or would that embarrass him? Was it better to pretend I never saw it? While I'd dithered over the decision, he'd reached the bench and restored his dignity himself. But it was clear to me what he'd needed—elasticated sweatpants that would stay on.

At Family Dollar, I'd spent twelve dollars on three pairs of sweatpants, discounted to four dollars each. Two for Mr. Esposito, one for myself.

I pulled out my phone, hoping to see a text from Shai, but my battery had run out. Raindrops slid down the dark phone screen, and I shoved it back into my pocket. These cheap sweatpants were comfortable enough, and they had pockets. I was starting to think I wouldn't wear anything else.

Mortana liked glamour. I wanted to wear pajamas all day. Not much of a life plan, maybe, but right now, I didn't have a better one.

After I dropped off these sweatpants, I'd get a bus to my favorite part of town, the historic district around

3

Osborne Common, and splurge on a hot chocolate in Ye Olde Osborne Coffee Shoppe. Situated northeast of here, that part of the city boasted Georgian houses, quaint brick sidewalks, cobbled roads, and signs with pristine gold lettering. And while I was lifting my spirits there, I'd dry off, pull out my little notepad, and come up with my master plan.

When you had only a few dollars and half a box of cereal left, you really needed a plan.

I turned onto Gallows Hill Road, walking quickly. Colored flags fluttered in the wind, adorning an over-grown parking lot that had once been a used car dealer-ship. The sky was growing darker now. Across the street, the broken windows of a mint-green concrete building had been boarded up with plywood. Just beyond that sat Mr. Esposito's ramshackle house—chipped white paint, a garden of weeds and tall grass, and a curtain hanging halfway down the front window. I really needed to come back here and help with the house a bit. No one else lived around here or kept an eye on him, and he didn't have any family.

The gate in the chain link fence was open, and I crossed through. I climbed the steps onto the front porch, where Mr. Esposito stored his cans and newspa-pers. On the porch, water dripped through the overhang onto rotting wood.

As I waited, shivering, I listened to the shuffling behind the door, accompanied by the sound of a walker hitting the wooden floor.

Even if my magic was fading in the mortal world, I

4

could still hear like a demon. Was this why my mom had always seemed to know everything I was up to? I couldn't get up in the night to check my phone without her overhearing it.

After a few moments, Mr. Esposito opened the door. His thick white eyebrows crept up his forehead, questioning, and he peered at me through his glasses. "Rowan!"

I held up the bag of sweatpants. "I brought you something, Mr. Esposito. I accidentally ordered a bunch of men's sweatpants, and they don't fit. I thought they might fit you. I'm too lazy to mail them back, you know?"

"Oh." He smiled. "That's nice of you to think of me."

Mr. Esposito and I were alike. Neither of us had any other friends in Osborne, and we could barely manage getting through normal life without a series of disasters befalling us. When we had nothing to do, we sometimes ended up at a coffee shop for chess. He played slowly and deliberately and was a million times better than me.

With a shaking hand, he took the bag from me and gave me a feeble smile. "Do you want to come in for tea?"

The warmth sounded nice, but he looked exhausted. "I've got to run, but thanks. Chess soon?"

He nodded. "That would be lovely, Rowan."

I watched as he tied the plastic bag around the top of his walker. "You should get out of the rain. Night is falling fast." He frowned. "I don't think it's a good night for you to be out." His eyes became unfocused, his forehead furrowed. "Rowan, I think...there's something... something's not right."

Maybe he could tell I was a demon now. "Yeah. It's grim weather, isn't it? I'll see you soon, Mr. Esposito."

I waved goodbye as he scooted back to shut the door.

As he did, I felt the hair rising on my nape. My demon instincts screamed that I was being watched by a malign presence.

Orion?

CHAPTER 2—ROWAN

*F*or one moment, I thought—hoped?—that it was my former incubus friend. Maybe he'd realized his mistake. Maybe, any minute now, I'd be back in the City of Thorns, looking out at the Atlantic.

But when I turned around, I found something much worse than Orion hurtling down the sidewalk. Five demon hunters were headed toward me, each one wearing the little hammer insignia of the Malleus Daemoniorum—Hammer of the Demons.

They stopped at the fence's opening, blocking me in. Jack was among them, along with his dad—an older, white-haired version of him who I'd seen in political ads. I was pretty sure I recognized two of the other guys from Jack's fraternity—large, red-cheeked men in white baseball caps, Patriots sweatshirts, and beaded necklaces. Basically interchangeable, except that one of them was drinking a beer. They didn't look threatening, and yet—

"Is this her?" Jack's dad asked quietly, his voice

sending a shudder up my spine. He took a step closer onto the crumbling footpath. "Is this the one you saw in the City of Thorns?"

"Congressman Corwin." I cleared my throat. "Nice to meet you." I glanced to the right, wondering if I should run that way to leap the fence. Right now, they had me blocked in.

The fastest way, I thought, might be to the left—over the fence and into the driveway.

The congressman wore a navy blazer with a bright red tie. His hair was slicked back. He didn't seem to notice the rain picking up, drenching his neat hair. Over his shoulder, he carried a leather satchel.

Behind him, Jack nodded. "That's her. She seemed to know the other demons. They thought she was one of them. I said she wasn't."

The congressman took another step closer. I considered calling for help, but the only help available to me would be Mr. Esposito and his walker. If I knocked on the door and tried to get inside, there was a good chance these guys would follow me in.

Right now, my phone was dead in my pocket, so there weren't many options.

The congressman's nostrils flared as he sniffed the air. With a cock of his head, his jaw tightened.

Lightning cracked the dark sky, and my stomach clenched.

"Nice to meet you, but I need to go, so…" I trailed off.

I bounded down the stairs and ran for the fence. The jagged metal top cut into my palms as I leapt over it. I landed hard on the driveway, stumbling. But as I tried to break into a run, one of the frat boys blocked my path. Towering above me, he shoved me *hard*, slamming me onto the wet pavement. As I scrambled back to my feet, the rest of the guys surrounded me.

The younger ones parted, and the congressmen crossed over to me. Lips curling, he gripped me by the shoulder, his fingers clutching me tightly. He sniffed the air again, eyes gleaming with anger. "*Jack?* I thought you said she was mortal."

Adrenaline started to pump. *Shit.* I wondered how much magic I had in my system right now. Three days outside the City of Thorns—was I still stronger than a mortal at all?

I smiled blandly. "I *am* mortal, of course." I blinked innocently. "It's not my fault the demons kidnapped me. Ask your son. He was there. He told them all I'm mortal, and that's how I ended up here in Osborne again, where I belong."

Narrowing his eyes, Jack moved closer. He inhaled deeply, his face growing red. "She smells different now, Dad. She was mortal before, but she's changed. How was I supposed to know they could change?"

I swallowed hard. "Can you both stop sniffing me? Also, can you…" I paused, trying to think of a polite way to say *fuck off*. "Fuck off," I blurted. "Please."

The congressmen let go of me and opened his little leather satchel. "Are you sure she was mortal before, Jack?"

"I'm sure," he replied.

9

"The problem is, son, you're usually dead fucking wrong about things," his dad shot back, shocking me. We agreed on that, at least. "I want to take her alive for an interrogation."

My heart thundered. I didn't know precisely how demon hunters interrogated demons, but I had a strong suspicion it involved a whole lot of torture. "I'm going to have to decline that invitation, Congressman Corwin. I'm trying to cut down on the amount of time I spend being kidnapped and prodded with knives."

"I'm not asking." He reached into his bag and pulled out a metallic hook. It took a moment for me to register exactly what it was. Mortals didn't have claws like demons to carve out hearts, so they used implements instead. The sight of the instrument—like a small metallic scythe—sent a shiver of ice through my bones.

I hadn't actually tried to control my claws yet. Right now, I wished I'd been practicing that for the past few days instead of drinking boxed wine in a basement.

I moved to the left, trying to get around the hunters, but the congressman knocked me back again, and my head smacked against the pavement. Pain shot through my skull, and along with it, fury. I gripped my head, anger simmering. These could be the very people who'd murdered Mom.

Now my demon side was starting to rise.

Blocking out the pain in my head, I leapt to my feet and lunged forward. I landed my punch, but it didn't do much damage. The congressman slammed his fist into the side of my head again, sending me staggering back, and I hunched over, dizzy.

The blows were clouding my thoughts. I had nowhere to go. Orion thought I was Mortana and wanted me dead. The demon hunters wanted me dead.

Even a life of quiet desperation wasn't in the cards right now, playing chess with Mr. Esposito in Ye Olde Osborne Coffee Shoppe.

A wild, furious sort of panic gripped me, and I rushed forward, shoving Jack's father hard into the guys behind him. He fell back. I tried to make a run for it again, but Jack struck from the side, punching me in the head. I staggered as he moved behind me and threw my elbow into his ribs, and he grunted in surprise.

Right now, I might still have some demon strength and magic, but not a lot. If I'd been at full capacity, this fight would have been over.

One of the hunters lunged for me, swinging a glass beer bottle at my head. My hands shot out and blocked his arm, redirecting the strike of the bottle against his own forehead. Fragments of glass littered the rickety stairs.

He was down for now, but they were all around, one after another coming for me.

Jack was up again. He reached for my throat, and I dodged him, jumping to the side. He lost his balance and fell forward. I grabbed him from behind and slammed his head down on the jagged top of the chain link fence.

"Demon!" Jack's father hissed. "We will rid the earth of your kind!"

I spied an opening between the congressman and one of the others. *Now's my chance.*

But as I started to rush past him, the hook caught me in the side, ripping open my skin. Pain carved through me, and panic sunk its claws into my heart.

Oh, fuck, oh, *fuck.*

I gripped my side, freeing myself from the hook with a sharp tug. Grimacing, I fought to keep my thoughts clear. I couldn't die here...

A voice sounded in my mind, echoing as if it were coming from somewhere in the distance. *You must have a chance at the crown. Chaos. Chaos. Chaos.*

Was I hallucinating?

I stumbled into plastic bins, blood rushing from me.

I was going to die surrounded by enemies, bleeding all over Mr. Esposito's trash cans.

CHAPTER 3—ROWAN

*S*taggering, I fought through the pain. They could have killed Mom, and I couldn't die before I found out.

It was like a part of me had never left the woods. A part of me was still there, running through the trees, senseless with fear. A double version of myself, permanently trapped in the past. And only that part of me could remember exactly what happened. I had no idea who it was.

That night, I'd split in two. One part of myself would always be hearing her scream.

"Was it you?" I shouted.

No answer. The congressman took a step closer and gripped me hard by the throat, lifting me into the air and crushing my windpipe.

"What do you think, boys?" He grinned. "Should we still take her alive?"

I tried summoning my power, but I felt it sputtering

within me, struggling to ignite. Snuffed out again like charcoal doused with water.

"Alive, yeah," said one of the frat boys.

The congressman dropped me hard, and I gasped for air. "Did you kill my mom?" I rasped.

He brandished the hook. "I might have."

A bit of lingering demon magic crackled between my ribs, then started to heat, surging along my arm. With an electrifying burst of energy, I whirled and landed a hard punch in his face.

His head snapped back, but he recovered fast and swung for me again with the hook. This time, I managed to block it, gripping his wrist before he could rip me open.

I snarled at him, growing feral.

He bared his teeth. "Your kind have been a plague on our great nation for centuries."

Blood was pouring from my side, and my brain swam with dizziness, my mind dancing with the memory of what Orion had told me. He'd loathed the mortals more than anyone, believed they had no mercy when it came to demons.

Strength was seeping out of me, and my mind grew dark. As I faltered, the congressman kicked me hard in the stomach. The blow ripped my side open a little more, and I stumbled back, shocked by the pain.

"What do you want from me?" I muttered.

His lip curled. "Demons like you are wild animals. Predators. And do you know what we do to dangerous animals? We lock them up so they can't hurt anyone.

Sometimes, we hang trophies of your heads on our walls. A message to the others." He cocked his head. "I'm not sure you'll make it that long, though. A dying animal will find a dark corner to die in. You feeling that right now, demon?"

I *did*. My strongest instinct right now was to curl up behind Mr. Esposito's trash cans like a sick cat crawling off to die alone. With rising terror, I gripped my waist and stared at the blood pouring from me onto the driveway.

My mind flickered with memories of Mom's face, and I wanted to see her now more than ever. I stepped back, and my attacker slashed at me again, ripping the skin on the other side open. The screaming in my mind went quieter. I looked up at the congressman, taking in the smug curl of his lips. He was *enjoying* this. Blood dripped from his hook onto the pavement, a glistening pool of crimson.

Something snapped in me, and a burst of fiery magic sizzled between my ribs.

"You're right, Mr. Corwin," I snarled. "I *am* a predator."

Volcanic heat pooled in my chest and blazed down my arm and along my fingertips. I gripped the hunter's wrist as he swung at me again, the last vestige of my magic igniting in a burst of hot blue flame on his arm.

He screamed as his navy jacket caught fire. The flames licked at his face, and he dropped his metal hook, which clanged on the sidewalk. The smell of burning skin and hair nauseated me, but as much as I'd wanted to fight back, I wasn't going to watch someone burn to death.

I snatched the hook from the pavement and, with the last of my energy, slashed the congressman's throat. One quick swipe to his jugular, and his agony was over, his screams silenced. He fell to the ground, his body burning as the flames blazed higher. The other demon hunters screamed, stumbling over themselves to get away from me. They took off at a sprint down Gallows Hill Road.

The last of my magic drained from my body, and my legs felt weak. As bile climbed up my throat, I stepped past the burning body. I hoped the rain would put out the fire soon.

Mouth dry and body cold, a horrible thought struck me. I'd just killed a congressman. Lit him on fire and slit his throat. Right here, in Mr. Esposito's driveway.

Holy *fuck*. I wanted to lie down on the ground, but if I stuck around, I'd be arrested. What's more, if I went to the hospital or called an ambulance for myself, I'd be arrested.

Dizzy, I found myself shambling toward the road. I couldn't survive without medical help.

A voice called out from behind me, and I turned to see Mr. Esposito standing in his doorway, his figure hazy through the black smoke curling off the congressman's body.

"I'm sorry!" I blurted, unable to manage a full explanation.

Coughs racked his body for a moment, and then he shouted, "Rowan! Get to the City of Thorns!"

Another spasm of coughing shook his frail frame.

"Wait a minute. What?" He was right, of course, though I had no idea how he knew. As soon as I got within the city gates, my body would start to heal.

"Get to safety, Rowan," he said, and closed the door.

I could feel it now, too—an instinct, a tug between my ribs that pulled me east, toward the hill. My body had gone into survival mode, dragging itself toward the city, while I barely retained consciousness. That's where my body had been urging me to go, the City of Thorns, not behind the trash cans to die.

I moved faster, my legs carrying me through the shadowy streets. But mentally, I was starting to become delirious. Despite my injuries, my mind heated with memories of Orion's beauty—his pale eyes, high cheek-bones, and sensual lips. His thickly corded muscles—

Why in the name of all that was holy was I thinking of that right now?

I was dying, and all I could think about was how much I wanted to sit in his lap. How it felt to have his lips graze over mine, his thumbs brush over my breasts. Heaven help me, I wanted to rip his clothes off and run my tongue over his chest. It felt like he was here right now, like I could reach out and touch him.

What the hell?

Take it off. Now. The memory of those words from him made an ache build inside me, a bittersweet pang that had nothing to do with my wounds.

I wanted it to happen again.

That's what you think about at a time like this?

What was this, some last desperate craving for life as I was about to expire?

I looked down at the trail of blood on the sidewalk, and realization dawned. Of *course*.

I was a succubus now. Sex wasn't just sex to a Lilu. Sex was *life*. It was healing and strength.

Sex would save my life.

I turned onto Walcott Street. I had two options now —find some random guy and make him kiss me, or make it the rest of the way up this hill.

Knowing what the men were like around here, I decided to take my chances with the hill.

But once I got into the city, what then? Orion still believed me to be Mortana, his worst enemy, and that was a serious problem. If I got anywhere near him, I had a horrible feeling he might try to kill me. True, something had stopped him before, but he'd literally made a blood oath to kill me, an oath he was compelled to keep.

And not just me. Orion was obligated to kill everyone in Mortana's family.

I didn't think I was Mortana, but whoever I was, I was probably related to her. After all, she looked exactly like me.

As my head swam with these thoughts, I realized I'd made it almost halfway up the slope, my blood mingling with the rainwater flowing downhill. Orange light from the streetlamps glittered off the dark puddles.

My thoughts were going dark, and I considered resting in the grass by the sidewalk, but as sirens wailed in the distance, I made my feet continue. I gripped my stomach, trying to stanch the bleeding. Blood seeped between my fingers. Across a wide street, the gates of the demon city emitted a pale, golden light, drawing me closer. The towering gates were wrought iron, twisted in the shape of thorns and vines, with a golden skull in the center.

Behind me, the sirens blazed louder, and red and blue lights flashed.

Moving faster, I dragged myself across the street. Police lights strobed, and I slumped against the gate.

Fuck. How did I open it?

The police bellowed behind me, screaming at me to freeze.

With tears stinging my eyes, I pressed a single bloodied hand against the golden skull.

A gunshot rang out, and a bullet seared my thigh. At that moment, the key symbol on my arm began to burn. Rays of golden light beamed from it, mingling with the gate's light. The pain ebbed, and the gate unlocked. I tumbled inside, and the gate swung closed behind me.

Weeks ago, I never would have imagined it, but now this place felt like home.

CHAPTER 4—ROWAN

*I*t was like I'd been drowning and had finally come up for air. As soon as I crossed the threshold into the City of Thorns, I felt the healing shimmer over my limbs.

I lay on the brick, the magic already starting to replenish in my body. The wounds in my side were knitting, and the bullet was working itself out of my thigh muscle, but I didn't want to lie here forever. It seemed mostly empty here, but I could hear a few demons talking nearby. If I were seen, word would quickly get back to Orion.

I stood, trying to get my bearings. I hadn't come through the main gate before. When I'd entered the city before, I'd been unconscious, and I'd left half-delirious through a tunnel system.

For the first time, I surveyed the city's entrance, a little stone courtyard I'd wondered about for many years. The entire place—the streets, the alcoves, the ornate turrets—was built of the same beautiful honey-colored stone as the exterior walls. Across the courtyard, a castle loomed. A carved lion overlooked enormous wooden doors, crisscrossed with iron and studs.

In the other buildings around me, arched windows overlooked the courtyard. Narrow alleys jutted off from the square—some with stairs that continued farther up the hill, some with stone walkways overhead. Luckily for me, it was raining heavily, and almost no one was out tonight.

I stumbled toward the narrowest alleyway, finding it dark and abandoned. Rain pattered down, and thunder boomed.

As I walked, I ran my finger over the deep, fresh scar in my side. The wound didn't hurt at all, but it hadn't healed as much as I'd expected.

I kept moving until I found a small, dark garden with a fountain, like a tiny public park. Water flowed from stone serpent mouths, and ancient-looking runes had been engraved along the side of the fountain. Pale pink roses grew around it, scenting the air with their sweet perfume.

Looking for the driest patch, I curled up in the grass under a bench. I hugged myself, imagining a warm bed, and listened to the gentle sound of running water.

My eyelids grew heavy. Back in my true home once more, a blanket of sleep swept over me.

I AWOKE in the little rose garden with my clothes drenched. Best I could figure, I'd slept for an hour or two, and the rest had done me good. I felt better than ever, completely energized, and ready to take on the world. Did I like having demon magic? Hell, yes. I never wanted to leave this place again.

I exited the courtyard and found my way out of the network of alleys, reaching the river. As always, the air in the city was warm and humid, but the rain had kept the streets mostly clear. Nevertheless, I lurked in the shadows as I walked, not wanting anyone to notice me as I made my way back to my parents' house.

I followed the river east through the Sathanas Ward, filled with buildings adorned with carvings of monstrous heads and empty temples to the demon of wrath. Passing a windowless jail with an enormous iron door and a scaffold for executions, I soon reached the Asmodean Ward, the quarter once inhabited by the Lilu. At the easternmost edge of this section, the buildings thinned, and the river branched off into tributaries. There, I found my parents' dark mansion. It stood on flat ground against the river. Gothic gardens spread all about the property. Mist twined around a crumbling stone wall that surrounded part of their land and billowed around the mansion itself.

I swallowed hard as I entered the outermost edge of the gardens and made my way down a gravel walk, meandering between broken statues and thorny plants.

Wind howled through gnarled tree branches on

either side of the path, and the scent of the nearby sea hung heavy in the warm air.

My feet crunched over the wet pebbles. I glanced up at the gargoyles, visible now through the fog. All I really knew about this place was that Mom had lived here, and Mortana, too, long ago.

And that Mom's husband might have burned to death right where I was walking now. He was my dad, or so I assumed.

A tragic presence clung to the façade, and I shivered, looking back at the place where a burned body had been found. Another indication, I mused, that it wasn't me who'd killed Mom. Maybe not the Hunters, either, since they couldn't enter the city.

A buried, molten anger rose to the surface, a searing heat that burned my forehead. Before me, rays of light tinged the mist with gold. A gust of wind blew the fog away, and when I looked down, I saw it—the symbol that had haunted my nightmares for years—the five-pointed star reflected in a puddle.

My heart beat faster. A memory buried in the recesses of my mind stirred, but I didn't want to see it.

An eerie, forlorn wind rushed over me as I climbed the steps. Crossing between the columns, I paused with my hand on the front door.

When we'd come here a few days ago, Orion had said that the City of Thorns wasn't like the mortal world. Here, the air was imbued with magic, and memories lingered tangibly. Tragedy wrapped itself around the wood and marble, hanging like a bitter, heavy miasma. The hair stood up on my nape.

The door was still open a crack from the last time we'd run out of here—when I'd fled the building. I pushed it open wider and stepped inside, standing once more among the cobwebs and smashed busts of my relatives. Sighing, I glanced up at the high ceiling adorned with faded paintings of vines and ripe fruit.

Eerie, yes, but I was glad to be here alone. This time, I could explore without Orion looking over me.

Loneliness cloaked the mosaic floor of blue and gold and the murals on the walls. Sadness tightened my chest, and I found myself hurrying up the creaking stairs.

When I reached the third floor, I walked slowly through the halls, stopping to peer into a bedroom with deep green paint, chipped by the passage of years, and a canopy bed of faded red material that smelled musty and stale. Moonlight streamed through an enormous pair of balcony doors.

My eye caught something I hadn't seen before—a portrait hanging on the wall. I'd never seen the face in the painting, but recognition hit me like a fist. I hurried inside, transfixed by the image, the likeness of a man with high cheekbones, dark eyes, and shocking red hair, nearly unnatural in its color. Red hair the same shade as mine, blending to blond at the tips, curling down around his chin. The image in the frame filled in all the missing pieces, the differences between mom and me. There was no doubt in my mind that he was my father. I felt a lump in my throat as I read the name below the portrait: Duke Moloch.

Orion thought Moloch had been burned just outside.

I ran my fingertips over the name engraved on the gold frame, wishing I could have met him just once.

And as I touched his name, my mind ticked over the words in the nursery rhyme that I'd found here last week.

The Maere of Night
gave girls a fright,
but one queen loved him well.
He lost the throne,
but seeds were sown
in the garden of Adele.

Was this about Orion?

Whoever had written that poem had intentionally cloaked the real meaning. Why had this poem popped into my mind just now? I stared up at my father. As the words played in my mind again and again, a thought took root.

This was a poem about a Lilu male—a Maere of Night. My father had been one, of course.

My gaze lingered over his fiery hair, and I wondered if I'd gotten my fire magic from him.

He lost the throne...

My father was the true son of the mad king Azriel from the old days. He could have been the heir, but he lost out to Nergal.

Seeds were sown in the garden of Adele...

Adele was King Cambriel's mother—Nergal's wife.

And the seeds? Okay, I did *not* want to think about my newly discovered father's semen, but I'm guessing those were the seeds.

I shuddered, thinking of King Cambriel's cold beauty, his long, pale hair, his high cheekbones...

Like my dad's.

Dark eyes like ours. If you took Duke Moloch here, gave him blond hair...

Yeah, he'd look a lot like King Cambriel.

Had my dad knocked up Cambriel's mom?

I started pacing the room, and the old floorboards creaked beneath my feet.

If all that was correct, then Cambriel wasn't the true king at all. He was my half brother. My lip curled. Had he realized that when he'd leered at me?

He was someone with a rare fire power, like mine. Someone who could have lit Moloch on fire. Someone who could have burned Mom to death for knowing his secret.

I swallowed hard, my heart rate speeding up. Orion also had fire power. *Please tell me he's not also a relation.*

I sucked in a deep breath. Turning, I began to pace again, my hands shoved deep into the pockets of my damp sweatpants.

Orion had the mark of Lucifer. Unlike Cambriel, he was destined to rule—and only someone like that could murder a king.

The wind howled through the cracks in the old windows, and I pivoted again. The pieces of the puzzle were starting to slide together in my mind.

Orion had wanted me to identify Cambriel's magical protection, the thing keeping him alive. But a true king wouldn't need that. A true, destined king could only be killed by an heir.

That was Orion's plan, wasn't it? Orion had said he'd been blackmailing Cambriel. Now I knew why. He knew the king was no king at all.

Orion knew that *he* possessed the mark of Lucifer.

And as soon as he figured out what kept the king alive, he would kill him and take the throne for himself.

I crossed my arms as I paced and tried to remember the rest of the nursery rhyme. I had a photo of it in my phone, but the battery was still dead, so I closed my eyes, seeing the words in my mind's eye.

A Swindler king,
a golden ring
to keep his heart alive.
Take the ring,
fell the king.
The city yet will thrive.

My eyes snapped open. That was pretty clear, wasn't it? A golden ring.

I ran the words over and over in my head, certain that my parents had given me the secret to killing the king.

If the king took his rings off, he could be killed.

I bit my lip, wondering if this was why my parents had died.

They'd known how to end Cambriel.

CHAPTER 5—ROWAN

I left the green chamber and went into the room with the portrait of my mom. Moonlight spilled through tall windows, bathing everything in a ghostly silver. I was still wearing damp, bloodstained clothes. Going to an enormous wardrobe on one side of her bed, I opened the doors and stared at her dresses. They were a little threadbare but mostly preserved by time, silk dresses with puffed sleeves, some with beautiful lace, others with ruffled collars. None of them looked comfortable. My gaze went to a short white gown with full sleeves and a rounded collar. It must be a slip, or maybe a smock, with delicately embroidered trim.

In any case, I'd be borrowing it from Mom. I pulled off my wet clothes, standing cold and naked, and slipped into the white dress. I stared down at the shift, trying to imagine Mom in this garment. For a moment, I thought I smelled her floral scent.

A lump had formed in my throat, and I swallowed

hard. I closed the wardrobe and turned to look at the room. Maybe I could stay here for a little while until I figured out a better plan. I'd avoid Mortana's old place, where Orion might look for me.

My curiosity sparked, I looked around the room, my eyes roaming over the dark wood and time-faded painted walls. It was so calm here, like a tomb. So different from the chaos I'd fled in Osborne.

I crossed back into the hall and wandered into an old bathroom with a copper clawfoot tub and cracked mosaic floors flecked with gold.

In here, I could definitely smell Mom's sweet, velvety jasmine scent. The ache of her loss bloomed in my chest. Her presence was so strong in this place that I could almost imagine her moving from room to room...

Mom used to hide things.

Important things. Her cash, a diamond ring, the checkbook. She had a drawer in the kitchen with a false bottom, where she tucked valuables.

I crossed over to a candle in a sconce on the wall and summoned a bit of fire magic, except I couldn't get it to rise. Staring at my hands, I bit my lip and tried to envision the flames. How did you make magic appear, I wondered.

I gritted my teeth, trying to force the fire up.

How did it happen last time? I envisioned my desperation...

My chest heated, and the warmth flowed down my arm and wrist and into my fingertips—exhilarating. But it was only the tiniest of sparks, like the lick of a match on my fingertip. I lit one of the candles, and the flame on my fingertip flickered out.

Warm orange light spread over the room, making me feel more at home.

Where would Mom hide something important here?

A desk stood beneath a window—the same one where I'd found the nursery rhyme. I crossed over to it and pulled open the drawer. With a hammering heart, I ran my fingers around its bottom, then slid my fingernails into it. I pulled up the panel—a false bottom—and stared down at a single piece of paper.

Written on the page, over and over, was one declarative sentence.

Long live King Nergal.

I pulled out the paper.

But why would anyone hide *that*—a simple statement of loyalty to the former king?

Disappointment twisted my heart. I ran my fingers over the handwriting. It wasn't my mother's elegant cursive, but rather a blocky, masculine text. Was this my dad's writing? Duke Moloch—the strange and unfamiliar name of a man who looked just like me.

Mr. Esposito sometimes said, "If you don't have a family, you don't have a life," which was a bit annoying, considering that neither of us had families.

I wanted something that belonged to my father. Since I had nothing else, I folded up the note and tucked it into my bra.

I turned back to the desk and slid open another

drawer. A hot, dry breeze rippled over me, scented with burnt cedar.

Oh, *fuck*. He was here.

Shock rattled through my bones as I felt his molten magic thrumming up my spine.

I whirled to see the Lord of Chaos standing in the doorway.

The other one with the mark of Lucifer. My beautiful nemesis. Maybe I shouldn't have lit the damn candle.

Amber candlelight danced back and forth over his golden skin, sculpting his cheekbones. He pinned me with his stare, a faint smile on his lips, like he was about to catch his prey.

The shock of his masculine beauty stole my breath. A lock of his silver hair hung before his pale eyes, and my heart clenched. Why was he so fucking pretty? It was an unfortunate distraction from the fact that he was my enemy.

"Mortana," he said, taking a step closer. The raw hatred in his tone sent ice through my veins. "I'd hoped never to see you again. Why would you come back here, knowing that I wanted you dead?"

I crossed my arms. "What can I do to convince you I'm not Mortana?"

He shook his head slowly. "It won't work this time. I've seen your demon mark."

I took a step back into the wall. "Have you been waiting outside this house, or what?"

Moonlight washed over his enormous body and the black T-shirt that clung to his muscled chest. My gaze roamed his thickly corded arms and his tattoo—the snake tied into a noose. He *loved* to intimidate, didn't he? That was his thing.

The sardonic smile on his lips quickly disappeared, and malice shone from his eyes. "I haven't been waiting outside. I woke up with a hammering heart and a suffocating sense of dread. For a moment, I wondered if I was in Hell, then I knew what had shaken me from sleep and filled me with this overwhelming sense of repulsion. *Your* rotten presence, drawing me closer. It was you—back in the City of Thorns, against all reason. You could have bought yourself a few more days, Mortana, if you'd stayed away. You probably could have run. But your arrogance knows no bounds. Don't you realize I swore a sacred oath to kill you?"

I glared at him, my body rigid with anger. "*My* arrogance? And yet, here you are, so certain you're correct when you are dead wrong."

A thorny silence stretched out between us. "If you truly believe you are not Mortana, it is because you have erased your own memory. You once told me about the very spell that could make it happen. You offered it to me."

Fuck. Frustration ignited. "No. I remember my life as a child. I remember sitting in my mom's lap and having a stuffed lion named Leroy."

"How adorable. Too bad those memories are not real."

The world tilted beneath my feet. "No. That's not possible." The idea that my whole life had been false was too disturbing for me to dwell on for longer than a moment. "Look, I don't know who exactly I am, but that's why I'm here in this house. I'm looking for answers. Maybe I'm Mortana's sister, but several hundred years younger."

"Hmm." He was as still as stone, and dark heat radiated from his body. He pressed his finger against his lips, his eyebrows knitted. "I suppose you also think you are both Lightbringers with the same mark from Lucifer, both with fire magic. Identical. Interesting theory. Except that's not how sisters work, is it?"

"I'm not her!" My voice rose.

"And if you were an identical twin," he went on, ignoring me, "you'd also be four hundred years old. But you say that you're not. Nor are you a mortal doppelgänger, clearly." He stepped closer, and I felt his sinister power thrum over my skin. "Sorry, love. I don't believe you, and I'm afraid the oath compels me to end your life."

My mind spun. I was back to square one with Orion. Now he was sure I was the one who'd tortured him and killed his family.

And—okay. He was right. Sisters didn't look identical. But my memories were so real, so specific. The nights I needed Mom to lie in bed and rub my back when I had nightmares. The time I'd pissed myself at Nina McCarthy's birthday and had to go home early. The time I'd chewed on the back of a pen in class, and it had exploded in my mouth. A messy kiss sophomore year with a boy named Jeff who played the bassoon.

It couldn't be magic—what the fuck kind of magical spell would make all that up?

33

I swallowed hard, my emotions churning like waves in a hurricane.

"There are two of us with Lucifer's mark," I said desperately. "Why couldn't there be three? Something strange has happened, hasn't it? There should only be one destined monarch at a time. Otherwise, it makes no sense."

No reaction to that line of reasoning, just a step closer from the Lord of Chaos.

Darkness slid through my bones, and I could hear my own heartbeat. I was going to have to fight back against this pure wall of muscle, or I'd be dead. I had to tap into that predatory side, like I had before with the demon hunters.

Apart from my slow and steady breath, my body went completely still. A breeze rushed through the cracks in the window, toying with my hair. "I can see that there's nothing I can say to convince you."

My gaze swept over his brutal snake tattoo, the tail formed into a noose. Its dark, sinuous lines curved over his muscles. Shadows seemed to billow from him as he loomed over me. Intimidation was his kink.

"Why don't you confess?" he purred. "Let it all out, Mortana."

My heart was pounding so hard I felt like it was making the walls vibrate. His intense gaze penetrated me like he was trying to memorize each curve of my features.

"Well, well, well," he said, his voice silky, "I see it in your eyes. Even you are not convinced. I can read the doubt there. You wonder if you're evil. You wonder if you're Mortana, and you simply cannot remember."

My fingers tightened into fists. "You're really starting to annoy me, do you know that? Always so confident that you're right."

Another slow step closer. "But do you know what I love?" he murmured.

"Let me guess," I shot back. "Yourself? Reading smut. Being a big scary incubus with snake tattoos?"

He was at my throat before I could finish the next sentence, and he swiveled me around, pressing my back against the wall. Somehow, he'd done all this without hurting me. His fingers laced around my throat, but they didn't squeeze.

His knee slid between my thighs, pinning me in place. His body was as heavy and solid as the wall behind me.

"Snake tattoos..." He let out a low chuckle, but I saw no amusement in his eyes. "Ah, lovely Mortana. You are easier to pin down than you once would have been. Fragile, almost. Breakable, slow, and weak. You've lost that fighting spirit. But it seems you remember something from the past. Let's go over why I got that snake tattoo, shall we?"

What the fuck was he talking about? Remember *what*?

I pulled at his wrist, trying to move his hand away from my throat. "I don't know what you're talking about. I can see the tattoo for myself—that's why I mentioned it. You like to intimidate, don't you? Big, scary demon boy."

His knee slid further between my thighs, and he stroked his thumb over the pulse in my throat, a languid, sultry movement that sent a strange, forbidden shiver through my body. What the hell?

His pale eyes were half-lidded, and he looked like he was in a trance as he gazed down at me.

Lowering his mouth to my ear, he whispered, "Confess, love. Let it all out. Have you been faking your memory loss? Do you remember everything? Do you remember the snakes?" He pulled back again to study my face, intently trying to read my expression. His eyes flickered, dark and heated.

I held his gaze. "No."

Slowly, his hand brushed down my throat to my chest. Heat radiated off his body, warming my skin. His face was close to mine, his breath ghosting over my lips. I could feel my cheeks flushing.

Long silver claws shot from his fingertips, and my heart skipped a beat. The tips of his claws were already piercing the thin fabric of the little white dress. All his muscles were rigid.

I couldn't tell if he was using all his strength to stop himself from killing me or to convince himself that he needed to.

Holy shit. The threat of imminent death sharpened my senses.

And I wasn't just Rowan the mortal anymore. I wasn't Mortana, either—but I was a fucking succubus. I had power now.

I reached up and touched the side of his face. "Orion," I murmured. "Why are you pretending to hate me?"

Nearly imperceptibly, his features softened. His eyes

grew dark all at once, and his lips parted. His claws began to retreat, but his knee remained firmly between my thighs.

I brushed my thumb over his lower lip. His sharp intake of breath did something to me, made my muscles go taut and my thighs clench around his knee. His midnight eyes swept down my body to linger on my breasts. I was sure he was remembering what I looked like naked, and for a moment, I felt like I was completely bare before him. I moved my hips forward a little.

Around us, the air grew humid, sultry, and I let my head fall back against the wall.

Entranced, Orion slid his hand higher again to cup my throat—gently this time, just below my jaw. Now, his touch was reverent. His thumb brushed over my lips like I'd done to him, and I took it in my mouth, sucking on it for a moment. Another sharp intake of breath from him.

That ice-cold expression had left his eyes, leaving behind a smoldering possessiveness.

This was the moment to act.

I slammed my forehead into his nose, and he dropped his grip on me, staggering back. I brought my heel down hard into his kneecap, buying myself some time.

Run, Rowan. That's what you do best.

Just when I reached the door, I felt his powerful arms wrap around me—one hand around my throat, the other clamping my arms to my sides. *Fuck.*

His claws were gone, but his iron body had me locked in a vise-like grip. Dread shivered through me. Something I'd said had flipped a switch in him earlier—the thing about the tattoo. Or something about snakes. Whatever it was, it had been exactly the wrong thing to say.

"You could be powerful, Mortana," he said quietly. "But I think you've forgotten how to fight like a demon. And in case your question was real, I don't know that I hate you anymore. I don't think I feel anything for you at all. It's hard to hate someone you no longer respect."

For a moment, his words hit me so sharply, I felt like I could hardly breathe. I don't think I'd realized until now how absolutely desperately I wanted things to be right between us. Because the sad truth was, I hardly had anyone else left.

"Is that so?" I tried to keep my voice steady.

"This new version of you has been nothing more than a tedious inconvenience. You are neurotic, dull, and unskilled at everything."

Rage erupted. I jammed my heel hard into his calf—once, twice. But this time, I had no effect on him. It was like slamming my foot into a stone wall.

Shit. That move killed in my self-defense classes.

I might be strong as a demon, but Orion was a force of nature, a demonic god hewn from stone and fury.

My heart slammed against my ribs. I shifted my body, trying to break free of his grip, but his arm only tightened around me.

The side of his cheek brushed against mine. "Mortana," he whispered. "It's not just the oath, or the fact that you murdered my family. It's not just your sadism. No, on top of all that, you are my rival for the throne. You are the other demon with the mark of the Lightbringer. You always knew I bore the same, didn't you? And that's precisely why you delighted in tormenting me in the dungeons."

I kept struggling against his grip, but I wasn't getting anywhere.

"You were the one who killed King Nergal, weren't you?" I said. "Only an heir could do it. I know it wasn't me. And that's how you blackmailed Cambriel."

"Good summary." His deep, languid voice betrayed not a hint of exertion. "And once I figure out what is keeping Cambriel alive, everyone will know that I'm meant to be on the throne. That I'm meant to be king."

If I could keep him talking, maybe I'd figure out a way to stay alive.

I turned my head, my cheek brushing against his. "But *are* you destined to rule? Or am I? It must make you wonder, since there are two of us."

His body was growing hotter. "You were born before me. I always assumed I was a correction of a terrible abomination."

When someone was delusional or psychotic, you couldn't argue with them outright. They'd just think you didn't understand them. You had to work within the boundaries of their belief system. "Fine. I was born first." I reached behind, sliding my hand under the hem of his black T-shirt, and stroked his abs, just above his belt. By the sigh he let out, I thought it was working. "The thing is, Orion, when I saw you in that bar in Osborne, you were desperate for one thing." I moved my hips against him gently and heard his intake of breath. "You wanted to know how to kill the king, because it's the only way the city will accept you as a ruler. Out of curiosity, have you tried to kill him before?"

"He comes back." His voice sounded husky, rasping. "That's how I know he's protected."

I rocked my hips again. "I know how to kill him now. If you kill me, you'll never know how to get him out of your way. You'll never convince the City of Thorns that you're the true king. Whether or not he was supposed to be crowned, he was, and you can't undo that unless he's dead. No one will accept you as king so long as he's alive. No one knows you're the heir. You need me."

There was a quiet chuckle from the wall of pure muscle behind me. "Oh, you know his weakness suddenly, do you? Why would I believe you?"

I stroked my fingertips under his shirt. My breath was shallow, heart racing. His magic curled around me, stroking my skin. "I'll make a blood oath. I'll tell you how to kill the king if you let me live. Everyone in the City of Thorns will know you're the true and rightful heir once you slaughter him. We both win."

"You forget something," he purred, stroking one of his fingertips over the pulse in my throat. Strangely, it made me shiver—but not from fear. "For one thing, I don't believe you'd willingly give up the throne. And for another, there is the oath. If I don't fulfill my promise, I will die."

CHAPTER 6—ROWAN

"*I* know there's a tiny spark inside your soul that tells you I might not be her."

The silence that followed told me that yes, I'd hit a mark. And maybe that was the only reason I wasn't dead yet.

"You certainly don't have the killer instinct she had," he said at last. "The thing is, love, I made this little promise to kill her whole family. I know you are related to her. So whatever way you slice it, I am bound to kill you. I can feel my heart constricting just standing here, touching you. Every moment I let you live makes me feel closer to death."

Desperation erupted in my chest. "There's got to be a way to undo the oath."

Another long silence spread out between us.

"There *is* a way," I said, and my fingers tightened on him. "I know there is. Sever the oath, and then I'll tell you what you need to know."

"The simplest thing would be to end your life." His eyes blazed with dark intensity.

But the question was, if he was so hellbent on killing me, why hadn't he done it already?

"It sounds like you're trying to convince yourself. You don't *want* to kill me." A mixture of fear and hope twisted inside me. "Something is stopping you. Why don't you start by admitting the truth to yourself? Some part of you actually *likes* me."

He lowered his hands, releasing me. "Every part of me loathes what you were. But no. You don't seem the same."

As I turned to face him, I tried to catch my breath. "I have information that you need. If I'm dead, you'd have to accept that Cambriel could be sitting on that throne for generations. If you kill me, you'll be murdering the one person who has the information you need. My parents were killed for a reason, and that was because they knew how to kill Cambriel."

Shadows stained the air around him like ink, and a warm breeze skimmed over my skin. My argument was a bit flimsy. Would it actually work?

He cocked his head. "Why don't you tell me how to kill the king, and then we will figure out how to break the sacred oath."

I crossed my arms "What is it about the past ten minutes of you threatening to kill me that makes you think I would trust you right now?"

Darkness spilled through his eyes, and he slid his hands into his pockets. His body language looked relaxed and casual, but there was real intensity in that midnight stare. "I need you to cut your palm and make an oath."

I looked down at my hand. "What, exactly, am I going to promise?"

"Two things," he said. "One, I need you to swear that you actually know how to kill Cambriel. If you're lying, you will die. Two, swear that you will tell me this secret as soon as I sever the oath. Agree to these conditions or forfeit your life."

I inhaled deeply. "I can't promise I can tell you how to kill the king because nothing in life is certain," I said. "I *can* promise you that I have a solid theory, one I believe is true and will share with you after you break *your* oath."

"Good. Slash your palm."

Holy shit, he was going for it. Maybe, deep down, he didn't want to kill me for some reason. I held out my hand. "Do you have a knife?"

His brow furrowed, and his claws shot out. "Just use yours." He raked a long silver claw against his palm, and crimson blood dripped onto the floor.

I looked down at my hands, willing my own claws to appear. I tried to imagine them gleaming from my fingertips.

After a few awkward moments, I looked up, meeting Orion's gaze. "How do I bring the claws out?"

He took a step closer, peering down at me. "You really remember nothing."

"Literally nothing of being a demon." I shook my head. "My claws and fire came out recently, but it sort of happened of its own accord."

"Was your life at risk at the time?"

My brain flickered with disturbing memories from earlier that night. Me, surrounded by enemies and bleeding by the trash cans. "Oh, yes. A group of mortals was trying to kill me."

The corner of his lips twitched. "Did you end their lives?"

"One of them."

"When your life is in danger, it provides a shortcut to your primal side. As a demon," he said, "you are part beast. A killer among prey. You need to remember how to connect to that side of yourself, to everything you've buried. To your pure, animal instinct."

The *id*.

I closed my eyes, trying to tap into the animalistic side of myself. I saw the congressman burning to death in the driveway and heard his screams. I smelled the smoke in my nostrils, and I wanted to be sick.

My eyes snapped open again. "It's not working."

"Try again, Mortana."

I narrowed my eyes. "Rowan. The name is Rowan."

A half smile. "Try again. I don't want your blood on my claws unless I'm ending your life."

With a deep breath, I closed my eyes once more and tried to summon my predatory side. Flames danced in the dark recesses of my mind, screams that pierced the silence.

I let out a long, slow breath. "I'll get a knife," I said quietly. "I'm getting sick of your mind games."

But before I could take a step away from Orion, he

spun me around and pressed me against the wall, dominating me with his powerful body. I was no match for his strength, and he was letting me know it.

"You know, Orion," I said through labored breaths. "I think I actually hate you more now than ever."

Instead of responding, he lowered his head and pressed his sharpened fangs to my throat in a pure, primal display of dominance—trapping me here, even as I tried to free myself.

"You're a big boy. Use your words!" I shouted. "For fuck—"

I broke off in shock as his fangs pierced my skin, drawing blood. The pain of it robbed me of my thoughts for a moment, drowning out my ability to speak. I snarled and shoved my elbow back into his ribs as hard as I could. Anger seared me, rushing through my nerve endings, incinerating my worries.

He released his grip on me, his eyes dark as ink.

"When you're shifting," he said, "you don't think in words."

I looked down, pleased to see my claws glinting in the moonlight, the golden light of my demon mark aglow.

Catching my breath, I drew one of my claws across my palm. Blood streaked across my pale skin and dripped to the floor.

Orion grabbed my bleeding hand and stared into my eyes. "Good. Now, repeat after me. On pain of death, I swear a sacred oath that I believe I have a strong theory of how to kill King Cambriel."

I repeated him, word for word, stating that I would

divulge the king's weakness as promised. I felt the magic of the oath skitter up my spine, and when the oath was done, I pressed my bleeding palm against his. He gripped my hand tightly, holding on with a firm grip. As our blood mingled, a vision started to burn in my mind.

I wasn't in my parents' house anymore, but in a dungeon with five large serpents...

Fear knocked the wind out of me.

The vision changed, and a body swung soundlessly from a gallows above me, her shadow moving back and forth over a silent pit. Her neck was bent, broken, and I could see that her eyes were still open—blue eyes, pleading. She was still alive. Terror choked me fiercely, like my soul was splitting in two.

Gasping, I pulled my hand away from his. I was shaking. "What the fuck?" I whispered, staring at Orion.

I was no longer in the prison but back in the mansion. I let out a slow, trembling breath.

He frowned at me. "What?"

I shook my head, trying to clear my head of the horrible vision. I wasn't scared of snakes, but those serpents had scared me half to death.

His eyes glinted. "You're mine for the next few days. That's about all the time I have before the oath kills me."

"There's something you should probably know. The entire Osborne police force is looking for me, and they might report me to the king. I broke the contract between mortals and demons when I killed someone."

"The king will probably find a way to sweep it under

the rug. And if he doesn't, let's burn that bridge when we come to it. Tomorrow, we leave to find the Dying God."

"Sorry, what?"

He arched an eyebrow. "We're going to Hell."

I stared at him. "Hell."

"Until we leave, I'm not going to let you out of my sight. As soon as I do, I know you'll run, so you will be with me every moment of every day until I get the secret from you. And as soon as I get that secret, you will leave the City of Thorns for good. You will no longer be allowed within my kingdom."

I glared at him. *We'll see about that, dick.*

Maybe I didn't want to live my life on ramen noodles in a basement anymore. Not to mention that I was a wanted woman in the mortal realm. *This* was my home.

I looked down at my palm, watching it heal. When I met Orion's gaze again, I straightened.

He was right about one thing. I *did* need to learn to be a demon. And everything he'd said to me tonight filled me with anger.

It's just hard to hate someone you no longer respect at all.

Screw you, Orion.

"Where are we sleeping, then?" I asked with a sharp edge in my voice. "Your place or mine?"

His expression was cold, almost bored. "Yours. I'd rather not be seen with you again. It was embarrassing enough the first time."

I wanted to scream. "Guess what, Orion? You're not the only one with a dead family, but you're the only one using it as a license to be an absolute twat."

47

He let out a short laugh. "The thing is," he said blandly, "I don't really give a fuck what you think. Apart from our one little tryst, I find you tedious and pathetic. And the truth is, I was only drinking from your raging lust because that's how I feed. That's all. I want you out of my life."

I was so furious now, my entire body was shaking with adrenaline. "And that lust? That was inspired by your incubus magic. Because there's absolutely nothing appealing about a miserable twat with interpersonal problems. You know what I think?" I continued. "The world would have been better off if you'd never left the dungeon."

Stony-faced, he walked past me. The pure vitriol of his words made me feel like my chest was cracking open. I could hardly breathe.

CHAPTER 7—ROWAN

*W*hat. An. Asshole.

So, I was only interesting as long as I fulfilled his incubus lust for sex? Clearly, there was no need to bore him by ever speaking to him again. The miserable fucker could have silence.

I clenched my jaw, trying to master my anger as we walked through the dark city streets slightly west of my parents' place.

When we finally crossed into Mortana's old apartment building, the human male who opened the door for me was a welcome sight. He grinned at me. His hair was as red as mine, and a smattering of freckles flecked his nose.

I crossed into the hall, my gaze roaming over the grandeur of the lobby. It was like an ancient, luxurious hotel, the floors tiled with blue and amber. Golden stone arches stretched high above us, and a staircase curved up to the mezzanine, where I'd find my apartment. My gaze drifting upward, I stared at the seductive image of Lilith and the snake curled around her body painted on the ceiling.

I sighed and turned back to the human. "Good to be home."

He beamed at me. "Lady Mortana. I wasn't sure you'd return, but I did hope I could tell my girlfriend I'd met you." He cleared his throat. "I've just started my internship here." He glanced down at the ground. "Sorry, I'm not supposed to speak to you."

Internship. In other words, the demons had convinced him to work for free. Orion would probably point out again that the demons learned their most evil shit from the mortals.

I flicked my hair over my shoulder, like Mortana would. "I suppose you can speak, mortal, since this weird stalker looming behind me isn't worth talking to."

His eyes darted between us, and he choked out a nervous laugh. "Okay, well…"

It was probably occurring to him that he, as doorman, should reject the stalker, except the stalker was six-feet-plus of pure muscle and ferocity.

"Doorman," I said imperiously, like Mortana, "don't worry about that idiot. I'll have coffee in the morning." I gazed over his shoulder at a fire extinguisher on the wall. "Did you bring that here?"

The mortal glanced back at it. "Just looking out for this beautiful old building. Since, you know…" He gestured to me, probably referencing my fire power. I could send this whole place up in flames at any moment.

"Right." I arched an eyebrow. "Nervous about fires, are you?"

He nodded vigorously. "Mortals can actually die from it. There are no fire alarms, and the building is definitely not up to code." His voice cracked as he spoke, and he looked at the ground again. "Is there anything else you need, Lady Mortana?"

I cocked my head, studying him. His suit looked expensive, but he hadn't gotten the hang of ironing his clothes properly because his white shirt was wrinkled. Obviously, he wasn't used to dressing up. Had I seemed such a mess when I'd been mortal? Shit. I had, hadn't I?

And that was only a few days ago.

I had a sudden overpowering urge to take him under my wing, to make sure he got paid for the work he was doing. To make sure no one took advantage of him.

"What's your name, mortal?"

His cheeks went red. "Carl."

Orion stepped forward, towering over both of us. "Well, this has been tedious as Hell, so we're leaving now."

My eyebrow rose again. "You really like that word *tedious*, don't you? Did you just learn it?" He definitely seemed annoyed right now. And considering how I now felt about him, of course I wanted to run with that.

I moved closer to Carl and leaned back against the desk. "I was actually getting to know Carl here. I think we'll be friends. He's *interesting*. You know, in our world, it's a novelty when someone isn't a terrible person. Have you ever considered that?"

A muscle twitched in Orion's jaw.

"So, Carl," I drawled, "sorry my stalker here is in such a hurry. He really doesn't understand fun at all. Not like us. Tell me, Carl, what are your interests besides smoke alarms and fire extinguishers?"

He swallowed hard. "Are you really interested?"

I shrugged. "Believe it or not, I happen to find fire safety fascinating, so you're off to a good start. It's been a while since I've met anyone I had anything in common with."

The growl that rumbled from Orion's chest was so quiet, I didn't think Carl's mortal ears could hear it. Maybe he was just impatient, but I could tell he hated that I was paying attention to the doorman.

Carl shifted from one foot to the other. "My hobbies. Okay. I like making tacos. And I'm an artist, mostly drawing with ink on paper. And I like history, like the witch trials, and beautiful old buildings like this."

Holy moly, he was like a male version of me.

"I've always been interested in the history of the Great Demon War—"

"The Great Mortal War," said Orion. "Mortals were the enemy."

Carl's eyes darted nervously between us. "But that was a long time ago. It's good that we're at peace now. We have so much to learn from each other, demons and mortals."

Orion shoved his hands into his pockets, narrowing his eyes. "Oh, I very much doubt that, Carl."

Carl didn't seem to hear him because he was staring

only at me now. "You're the last one, Duchess. The last of the Lilu. I read about what happened to your kind." His throat bobbed. "That must have been terrible for you."

I could feel the air heating, and the electric lights flickered. Was that Orion's magic?

"If you don't stop talking to this moron," said Orion breezily, "I will rip out his ribs."

Now Carl was paying attention to Orion. He let out a whimper and stepped back behind the desk, visibly trembling. He glanced at me, his lips pressed tightly together, and shook his head. I understood what he meant—he wasn't going to open his mouth anymore.

"Orion." I sighed. "You really should be locked up for the benefit of the rest of the city."

Schooling my expression, I waved my hand and said goodbye to Carl.

I let out a long, slow breath and crossed to the stairs, still not making eye contact with Orion. He was a much worse person than I'd thought—which was saying something, as we'd met when he kidnapped me and threw me in a dungeon.

My heels clacked over the mosaic floor as I walked toward the sweeping staircase.

I once thought Orion and I were alike because we both wanted revenge. But I only wanted to kill *one* person.

Orion? I had a feeling he wanted to burn the whole world down.

CHAPTER 8—ORION

I lay on Mortana's sofa, staring up at her ceiling. I didn't have a blanket because you couldn't exactly ask someone for a comfy blanket after you'd told them you hated them and wanted them dead.

I turned on my side, staring out the tall windows. The canopy of night spread above the pool outside. The window was open a crack, and I heard a barred owl crooning in the distance. On the other side of the pool, the Acheron River rushed past.

Even on the best of nights, I found it hard to sleep. Tonight, there was no way I could drift off.

When I thought of Mortana, it was like inhaling death, exhaling ash.

Rowan was different. Even if I *knew* they were the same person, it was hard not to think of them as the same. When she was around, embers smoldered to life in my chest for the first time in centuries, and I felt alive.

I hadn't woken with a feeling of dread and known she

was here. I'd had a feeling of warmth in my chest, dead charcoal sparking. Without Rowan, my world was cold, silent.

Unfortunately for me, everything about her was a lie. And that was because everything about Mortana had always been a lie, a deception designed to crush my soul.

When I'd seen the star of Lucifer blazing from her head, I'd known. It had all been a lie—another one of Mortana's sadistic tricks.

A humid wind whistled through the crack in the window. But that wasn't what was keeping me awake.

I didn't trust her, not enough to think she'd *actually* tell me Cambriel's secret, even with the blood oath. Deep down, she was Mortana, and Mortana always found a way out. I'd let her live, but only because I was too bloody weak to kill her.

It was hard not to think of the way Rowan moved, the way she'd touched my skin.

Who was she, really?

She was identical—*identical*—to Mortana.

And yet, she'd tried to save me from the bullets in that underground tunnel. Mortana would never have done that.

For a moment, there in the abandoned mansion, I'd been certain it had all been another one of her tricks. I was sure she remembered everything when she'd mentioned the snake, as if taunting me for what I'd done. Exactly like Mortana had, and how could she have known if she wasn't there?

I rolled onto my back, staring at the ceiling.

She was taking over every one of my thoughts. She was a wildfire burning through my skull until I could hardly think with my own words anymore.

Now, I could only hear the things she'd said. *Why don't you start by admitting the truth to yourself? Some part of you actually likes me...*

Letting her live was a betrayal to all the Lilu she had killed. One by one, they'd been led to their deaths in silence under the ground because of her.

Isn't there any tiny spark inside your soul that tells you I might not be her?

Fuck.

All I had to do was end her life. Instead, I was letting her sleep in the same apartment as me. Despite my oath to the dead, I was going along with her plan. She'd incinerated my own thoughts the first time I'd kissed her— back when we were supposed to be pretending, in the Temple of Ishtar. And now my mind wasn't my own anymore. She'd become my obsession.

Since I could not bring myself to kill her, the next best thing was to destroy whatever we'd had between us.

With several brutal insults, I'd burned it all. There you have it—a sacrifice on the altar of the dead. Maybe that offering would appease them for what I was doing now, failing in the mission they'd given me. I'd promised them I would kill her. I'd promised Ashur.

I find you tedious and pathetic.

I stretched my arms above my head and listened to the sound of Mortana rolling over in the bed upstairs. Was she having a hard time sleeping, too?

I kept thinking about the perfect curve of her ass in that sheer white dress, the way her hips swayed when she walked.

As a demon, she moved differently than she had before, smoother and more elegantly now.

Gods, I wanted her naked in my bed, but these thoughts were a betrayal to the dead, and I would no longer allow myself to indulge.

I clenched my fist, letting my claws pierce my palm to distract myself with the pain. I would think of the throne, the crown, nothing but the vengeance that had been my lifeblood. I absolutely would *not* think of her, or how it would feel to have her full red lips wrapped around my cock.

I closed my eyes.

Remember the past. Remember why you are alive.

Every morning, when I'd woken in the dungeon, I'd looked around at the four small walls of my cell. Before the mortals had come to arrest all of us, my father had given me a knife, and he'd taught me to whittle. I was little, but he'd trusted me with a tiny pocketknife. I'd been careful, so careful with it, my prized possession, and I'd used it to make sharpened sticks, which was about all I could do.

I'd had my pocketknife with me when we were arrested, and I'd thought I was getting away with something. I thought the guards had missed my little whittling knife when they'd searched me. It had taken me a while to realize the truth—they simply did not see me or my mother as a threat, not without our magic.

Before my mother was murdered, I'd made a birthday gift for her, whittled from a twig, a likeness of a queen with a lump for a head and ridges for a crown. I'd been thrilled with the idea that she would have a birthday celebration, even if it were in a cell. Each day, I'd ask her if her birthday was coming up, and she would say no. I suspect she'd seen me making the gift and knew I was excited about it. By delaying her birthday, she gave me something to look forward to.

"Soon, little one," she'd say. "Soon."

They'd killed her before I'd gotten the chance to give it to her. When I was twelve, they took the knife away.

After centuries down there, I could hardly remember my real name anymore. No matter. I only needed to remember vengeance, and so I focused on that one moment, the soul-shattering nightmare that had destroyed what I used to be and made me into a creature of revenge.

I became a new person—Orion, born in the dungeons. I'd named myself after the stars I could see through a crack in the stone—a constellation my mother had once pointed out to me. The old me had died.

And this, all of this, was the legacy of Mortana.

In the early days, there had been more of us. I was only a boy then, and I'd listen to them talk. Balthazar, Malphas, Saleos, Azazel, Marduk...each one of their names etched into my heart like a tattoo. Ashur lived in the cell next to me, and he would sing the old Lilu songs. I couldn't see him from my cell, but I remembered him from the City of Thorns, a towering, muscular figure with golden horns and long black hair. He'd worn golden cloaks, and his fingers glittered with jewels.

He'd always say we would avenge the Lilu, that one day, we would learn to fight back. We kept our families' memories alive by talking about each one of them. And some day, we would make our enemies pay, memorializing the dead in their blood. We would rip Mortana's heart out and stick her head on the gates. We would build statues to the dead.

We spoke of flames that would burn the city to the ground.

We didn't worship the gods down there, but rather at the altar of delusion.

And one by one, we'd hear the others led away, never to return. One by one, they left, their voices going silent, until it was Ashur and me, the last two.

Over time, Ashur's bravado grew quieter. His defiance started to bleed out of him.

For decades, we were completely forgotten. No one brought us food. At night, dreams of banquets tormented us. Food we could never eat, not even in our dreams. Then we'd wake, still starving, and remember where we were. I thought the hunger would last forever.

We turned into living skeletons, our intestines decaying inside us. I'd have eaten Ashur if I'd had the strength to break into his cell.

Ashur slowly lost his mind.

He forgot words to the songs. He asked me sometimes, plaintively from the other cell, to remind him of his name. He forgot his wife and children, and every one of the relatives he'd planned to avenge. Even when the guards remembered our existence and the food returned, his mind was gone.

Ashur was no longer. The man left behind spoke only in shrieks, refused to eat, even when he had food. The king saw no reason to keep a madman alive. At that point, death would be a mercy.

And that is how you kill someone with a clean conscience. You break them first, until they are no longer worth keeping alive.

When they took him away, I stuck my head through the bars to watch him escorted to the gallows. Ashur looked like a phantom from another world, bones and gray skin, and teeth that seemed strangely long in his emaciated face.

Our gazes met, and for a moment as they dragged him off, somewhere behind the madness, I saw a command to avenge him. And then he was just another name among the dead, one only I would remember.

It was my job to make this right.

Only I remained—the true heir.

But why was it always the least deserving who survived? Why did Ashur go, and my mother, and the beautiful succubus who used to give me apples—why were they all gone, and I was still here?

I knew why. I'd been blessed with a natural ability to kill quickly and easily. I was the one who would feed the Lilu graves with the blood of their murderers.

Outside, a flock of crows soared over the pool.

Mortana—Rowan—whoever—seemed to hate me now. *Good.*

But I still felt like her prisoner, thanks to that one tiny ember of doubt. That one spark of red light in the darkness—that question.

Was it really her?

CHAPTER 9—ROWAN

I listened as Orion climbed the steps, and my pulse started to race. Shirtless, he stood at the top of the loft stairs.

"What are you doing here?"

He crawled onto the bed, hovering over me. "I couldn't stop thinking about you."

Orion's hard, demanding body pinned me to the mattress.

I stared at up his beautifully sculpted face with what I hoped was an expression of pure hatred. He was, as he'd always told me, the worst person in the world. It was impossible to believe in a benevolent God when someone this hot was also this terrible, so that left only the demon gods who'd made him.

My gaze drifted to his sensual lips, and my cheeks flushed. He chuckled quietly, a dark purr that made my skin heat. Right now, it seemed nothing in the world existed but us, and I had his complete attention. He didn't find me boring at all now.

His smoldering gaze raked down my body, and his magic stroked my skin. "You're mine now," he said, his voice husky. His lips brushed over my neck, sending a forbidden thrill through my body. "Do you know how many times I've imagined claiming you?" he murmured against my throat.

Molten heat slid through my body. Each place where his body touched mine was sending forbidden shivers of pleasure racing through my blood.

"I don't care." I hissed. "I think you should know. I find you tedious and pathetic."

His thigh slid between mine, parting my legs—

An alarm sounded in my head.

No, not in my head. My phone was ringing. Well, that was good. I wasn't sure if the phone charger I'd found last night would actually work.

But who called on a *phone?* Who even had my number?

Orion wasn't here. I was lying tangled in the sheets of Mortana's loft apartment. Alone—which was good. The first coral rays of sunlight pierced the dawn sky, streaming into the room. What sort of sociopath would call this early?

I brushed my fingertips over the scar on my stomach, disappointed to find it still there. It definitely hadn't healed properly.

I picked up the phone and saw a missed call from Shai. She knew I hated talking on the phone.

I flopped back against the pillow. I needed coffee. Carl had promised coffee, hadn't he? I wondered if he'd bring it this early.

I rubbed my eyes. Orion was the worst, but even he wouldn't wake me with a phone call at dawn.

"Mortana!" Orion's voice rose from below.

"I won't respond to that name," I shouted back. "I mean, not after that."

"*Rowan*. I couldn't sleep. And while I was awake, wondering if I was making a terrible mistake, I noticed one of the king's spies prowling around outside. He was trying to hide behind a cypress tree on the other side of the pool. Does anyone know we're here?"

He was standing at the top of the loft stairs, shirt open and hair ruffled, not unlike the dream I'd just woken from, except this was much less fun.

"Does anyone know we're here?" I repeated. Finally, the fog of sleep cleared from my mind. "Only Carl. Why?"

"I'm just wondering why the king might be spying on you, and if someone has already alerted Cambriel." His eyebrows rose. "Hang on a minute. Who did you kill?"

"A congressman."

He frowned. "I don't think the king cares about mortal politics."

"He's also the head of the demon hunters. The Malleus Daemoniorum."

"Ah." His eyes glinted in the morning light. "They're the reason we are locked in this city. They continue to have power over this realm. Rowan, you chose the most inconvenient mortal to kill."

I pulled the sheet up over my tank top. "I didn't choose him. He came for me." I looked toward the window. "Why didn't the king come here first?"

"He'll be on his way from the Tower of Baal. We only have a few minutes to get out of here." He turned, bounding down the stairs. "I've got to take care of something before we go to Hell."

"What?"

The door slammed behind him.

My heart pounded. With my phone in my hand, I leapt out of bed and hurried down the stairs to change into fresh clothes.

At the wardrobe, I pulled on a long-sleeved black dress and a pair of boots. After zipping them up, I crossed to the window, shielding my body from view as I peered outside. Were there really spies outside? Cypress trees lined the riverbank, but beyond their trunks, I thought I saw figures moving...

What was Orion doing? Adrenaline lit up my veins.

I rushed over to the dresser and quickly packed a small leather backpack. What did one bring on a trip to Hell? I hoped my inability to burn would serve me well there.

Had Orion said something about a *dying god*?

I shoved a toothbrush and clean clothes into the bag. What if my magic powers didn't work in Hell? What if I *could* burn in the hellfire?

My pulse was racing out of control.

I grabbed my fire blanket, a small fire extinguisher, and my gas mask, and shoved them into the leather bag. I'd left the note from my dad on the kitchen counter, and I carefully slid that into one of the backpack's interior pockets for good luck.

Now *I* was ready to go, except I didn't know how to leave here without Orion.

My phone buzzed, and I flicked it on to find several texts from Shai. But it was the final text that made my heart skip a beat.

Any idea why I just got a summons to see the king?

Ah. So that's why she was calling. My heart thundered, mind whirling through the possibilities.

Of course. Jack knew I was friends with Shai. Jack would have told the king to go after my friend.

The Corwins had probably asked the king for my head on a platter.

Frantically, I typed back to her.

Shai. I need you to leave the City of Thorns.

I watched the three dots move across the screen with a growing sense of dread.

Are you kidding? I can't leave when I've been summoned by the king. Someone is coming to escort me.

My hands were shaking. If the king captured Shai, he'd use her to keep me here. As Orion pointed out, she was the only person I cared about. She was my leverage.

Hide, I wrote back. *Until I can tell you where to meet me. Orion will get us both out of here.*

Orion slammed open the door, blood spatter on his golden skin. I stared at him. "Who did you kill?"

Without a word, he strode up to me and took the leather backpack from my hands. Opening the bag, he removed the fire extinguisher and the other fire safety equipment.

"What are you doing?" I asked.

"We will have more pressing matters than fire where we are going."

He hurried over to the kitchen and pulled the fridge door open, then loaded my bag with snacks—cheese, fruit, and some bread from the counter.

"Grapes and Swiss cheese? That's more pressing than avoiding a fiery death in Hell?" I demanded.

"Swiss? Honestly. Comté is actually French, but it's a common mistake among the unsophisticated." He pinned me with his gaze, arching an eyebrow. "And you will find out why we need it soon enough."

I stared at the blood spatter on his neck again. "Are you going to tell me who you killed?"

"No one interesting." He dropped a bottle of water into the bag. "Just Carl."

My jaw dropped. "Of all the people to kill in this situation, you chose the harmless mortal nerd? The only nonthreatening person in the scenario?"

"Carl wasn't just an intern. He was spying for the king. When I took his phone, I found a text message to the king's spy agency letting them know you were here. But consider it an accident if it makes you feel better. My hands slipped, and I accidentally ripped off Carl's head and shoved his remains under the desk." He raised his eyebrows with mock seriousness. "Don't be so judgmental. It could happen to anyone."

"You ripped his head off," I repeated.

"On the plus side, he didn't tell anyone I was here, and now he won't be able to. Did any other demons see you last night?"

I was struggling to keep up. "I don't think so. No one was out in the rain. But the mortal police saw me enter the city."

"Shit. Okay. I can hear the army marching closer. We need to go before you meet the same fate as Carl."

My body buzzed with nerves as I slid my backpack on over my shoulders. "What's the best way out?"

"How well can you fly?"

I could fly…sort of, but Shai couldn't. I needed a path she could take, and I needed to make sure she could catch up to us. "Not really. Is there any other way?"

"I'll fly with you in my arms."

"You won't touch me," I said with venom.

A banging sounded at the door, and Orion went still.

I felt the air heating around me like a dry wind. Orion crossed to the window and slid it all the way open. He crawled onto the sill, his enormous body filling the frame —half out and half in. Outside, the rising sunlight gleamed on the swimming pool, so bright it was almost blinding.

I stared as he climbed through it, then perched on the sill. And then he seemed to fall.

CHAPTER 10—ORION

I touched down, then turned to look up at her, my beautiful nemesis.

Did she have any control over her wings whatsoever? She seemed to have forgotten everything about being a demon—how to shift, how to fight, how to instill fear into another person. In fact, she almost seemed afraid of herself.

Her red hair caught in the wind and the morning sunlight, like flames dancing around her. Was she going to jump, or was I going to have fly up there and get her?

Cypress trees surrounded the pool on three sides, giving us some privacy, but if anyone stopped to peer through the trunks and branches, they'd see us here. And the guards would break down that door at any moment.

At last, she leapt from the windowsill…and dropped like a rock, red hair streaming toward the heavens. She hadn't unfolded her wings and dropped right into my arms.

Instinctively, I held her tight, her heartbeat thudding against me. For a moment, I stared at her perfect mouth, and my mind brought up the memory of her lips parting against mine. She smelled like ripe cherries and the rich earth after rain. Heat sparked in my chest, embers of smoldering red. She was sexy as hell, no matter what she did or how much I hated her. And for an incubus like me, a woman like her was our lifeblood.

She glowered at me. "You can put me down now, dickhead."

Ah, good. She still hated me.

I let her down and started for the river. "Follow me."

Other demons in the City of Thorns hadn't spent over a century tunneling beneath the city. They had no idea what lay under our feet. It had taken me a long time to get from the dungeon to the old buried vaults, but once I had, I'd found a whole world underground—stone tunnels that had once been used for storing wine and food in the days before refrigerators.

I glanced back to see Rowan looking at her phone, seemingly unconcerned that the king might be handing her over to her executioners. She glared at me and shoved the phone into her pocket.

At the tree line, I looked in both directions, making sure no one was nearby. The sun slanted over the river, and the dark Acheron forest loomed on the opposite side. Cambriel's army had already passed by here. On the pavement beneath me, I could feel the vibrations of the king's army marching in the other direction. But soon, the soldiers would fan out across the city, searching every alley and alcove.

I found the vault covering, a round carving in the pavement marked with serpents, and lifted it. I climbed down into the darkness—not much of a jump down to the stone floor beneath—then looked through the opening, waiting for Rowan. She lowered herself, and I reached up to grab her by her waist, letting her down next to me. Then I slid the cover over the vault once more.

"This will get us out," I whispered. "Almost none of the other demons know the way around the vaults."

She still wasn't speaking to me. In the cold and wet down here, it smelled of the dungeons. In the dark, my mind slipped back again to the past.

King Nergal had capitulated to the mortals, and he'd learned his worst cruelties from them, the Puritans in particular. They taught him to terrify people. Break them, and they don't fight back.

When they'd marched us to the dungeons—the women, the children, the injured—they'd taken us past the severed heads of those slain. I saw my brother's head bleeding on top of a pike, and my father's. The mortals had done that.

That was the first time I'd felt something crack. When I saw their heads, I no longer knew exactly who I was because nothing was real anymore. The world had become a nightmare.

The thing was, for most people—even demons—it wasn't always easy to kill someone. If you recognized yourself in them, if you could see them as being like you, it was hard to end a person's life. This spark of similarity was protection, and Nergal didn't really *want* to kill all the women and children, the prisoners of war. That would be immoral.

That's why the king's soldiers had to change us first. Nergal had learned this from the mortals, too.

In Salem, they locked people in prisons. Most who went behind bars simply died there. Bodies full of lice, skin covered in lesions, gnawed on by rats. Those who survived were half-mad. And when it came time to kill them—I mean, they hardly seemed human anymore.

The Puritans, with their filthy prisons, had taught us how to control people. *They* taught us how to turn off empathy and get the results we wanted. Rowan liked to think empathy was a particularly human trait, but she was wrong. They could turn it off better than anyone. And when they wondered why they'd made me a monster, it was because they'd taught me to be strong.

The Puritans made people turn on one another, made them accuse their own family members. Mortana had learned that from them, and she'd suggested all this to the king—the dungeons, the mind games. And nothing breaks a person more than forcing them to kill their own family.

In the witch trials, the Puritans accused a little girl of witchcraft, terrifying her until she accused her own mother. The mother was hanged on Gallows Hill, and the little girl went mad.

To kill without guilt, turn your victim into a

gibbering wretch. Strip a woman to her waist, tie her to the back of a cart, and drive her through the streets to be flogged. Lock her up with mud and typhoid, and a child she can't feed. When the light is extinguished in her eyes, put out the rest, the sack of flesh and bones and self-loathing that remains.

This was *civilization*—a mortal invention.

But I was still here. I'd been marked as the Light-bringer, and even though I'd nearly drowned in darkness, my soul smoldered inside me—red embers in a sea of darkness.

I would make things right again.

CHAPTER 11—ROWAN

I followed Orion through the tunnels beneath the city, memorizing every turn. Water dripped down the vaulted stones onto my head and backpack.

While Orion walked ahead, I pulled out my phone and started frantically texting Shai. With just barely a single bar of reception, I wanted to make the most of it before it disappeared completely. So, I quickly told her how to find the vault, which turns to take underground, and to run as fast as she possibly could.

Shai was all I had left. She was my family now, and I'd protect her until my dying breath. And unlike Orion, Shai wasn't going to turn on me because I happened to be a demon.

Ahead of me, Orion opened the door into a larger tunnel, one with light streaming inside. I recognized this one. This was where I'd run, half in a daze, after I'd learned what I was. After the fire had spilled out of me for the first time.

I hammered out another quick text to Shai.

The tunnel opened beneath a stone underpass that looked abandoned, strewn with newspapers, old cans, and a broken refrigerator. An enormous dumpster hid the narrow opening into the demon world. The grimy setting would put anyone off investigating.

When we stepped out from under the old train bridge, New England's beauty was on full display around us. Leaves swirled around us, wine-red and pumpkin orange, the first signs of fall. Victorian brick buildings stood on either side of a curving road, lined by cars on the right side.

Orion looked in both directions, then crossed to a sleek, steel-blue BMW sedan parked at the bottom of a gently rolling hill.

Out of nowhere, a strange fear sparked in my mind.

What if he'd left his keys behind?

We left the keys behind, and it was my fault for distracting him—

I felt my blood go cold, then shook the fear from my thoughts as he pulled the keys from his pocket.

I walked over to the car, glancing back at the dumpster. I needed Shai to appear *now.* I flicked open my phone to find two letters—*ok.*

Orion hit the button to unlock the car and got behind the wheel. "Get in."

We were taking a hundred-thousand-dollar car to

Hell. Clearly, blackmailing the king was a lucrative line of work.

But Shai wasn't with us yet.

I opened the back door for Shai, mentally willing her to move faster.

Orion shot me a sharp look. "Rowan. Get in."

I slid into the front seat, and the hem of my dress rose to the top of my thighs. Orion's gaze locked on my legs, his eyes growing darker. The air around us heated. "Shut the doors." His low, masculine voice thrummed over my skin like a caress.

With a flare of warmth in my cheeks, I tugged down the hem of my dress.

He dragged his gaze to mine, then his focus moved to something over my shoulder.

I turned to see Shai burst from behind the dumpster. She sprinted over to the car and yanked open the back door. She caught her breath, her rich brown skin beaded with droplets of sweat. Jumping inside, she closed the door and started to buckle her seatbelt.

Orion stared at her. "Absolutely not."

I closed my door. "She knows I was in the city. Don't you want to cover our tracks? You can't murder her, too. Even if you wanted to."

She leaned forward. "Where are we going?"

"To Hell," he said quickly. "You might not like it."

She shrugged. "Can't be worse than Albany, and I nearly went there for college." She pulled an apple out of her bag and bit into it. "Speaking of which, can we discuss how I can get back into Belial University after this? Because it seems like I'm going to be kicked out."

I belted myself in, my mind whirling. Was Hell *actually* real, or was this a metaphor?

But we hadn't started moving yet, and Orion's eyes darted behind me again. He cursed under his breath and leapt out the door. I turned to see three demon soldiers running for us, their bodies flickering with blue and silver magic.

But they didn't get far. A great arc of fire burst from Orion's hand. Flames engulfed the soldiers, and they staggered around, screaming, smoke billowing from their bodies.

"Rowan." Shai's voice seemed to come from a distance.

I couldn't tear my eyes away. Shai was talking to me, but I could hardly hear her words. Bile rose in my throat.

"Rowan!" she shouted, shoving the back of my seat. "Don't look. Close your eyes and cover your ears."

She was right, of course. I leaned down, hands over my ears. I stayed there, hunched over, until Orion got back in the car and I felt the vehicle lurch into gear.

Slowly, I opened my eyes and sat up. Orion was speeding through the streets of Osborne.

"Okay, *what* is happening?" Shai shouted. "Why did Orion light those people on fire?"

Orion gripped the wheel hard as he took a sharp turn. "Is she why you said you couldn't fly? You wanted her to follow us?"

Well, he'd worked that one out quickly. "You wouldn't

have agreed to save her. You can't kill her, but you're not required to go out of your way to help her."

"Ah," he said quietly. "Of course. Everything about you is a deception."

I heaved an exasperated sigh. "Can we *please* just go to Hell in peace?"

Shai leaned forward again. "Does anyone care to fill me in? Why are we running from the king?"

I inhaled deeply before turning to look over my shoulder at my best friend. "The mortal demon hunters tried to kill me. And Jack was there. I killed his dad in self-defense, and now the king wants to hand me over because the mortals have some kind of control over our city."

"Shit."

Orion veered wildly onto Walcott Road, my old street, and I faced forward again.

He glanced at me. "Why do you look like you're about to vomit all over my beautiful car?" He sped through a red light at an intersection, and I gripped the car handle.

My mouth was full of saliva, and I swallowed. "I guess I have a thing about watching people burn to death. You know, the whole empathy thing. And your driving isn't helping the situation."

"Hmm, I'm not sure I believe you actually have empathy." He shot me an irritated look. "And I burned them because it was the fastest way to kill them. Now they won't report anything to Cambriel or the mortals. You're welcome." He careened left at an intersection. "Remind me again why I didn't kill you."

"Because even if you hate me, I'm the closest thing you have to a friend?"

Shai leaned forward. "Can someone please erase the memory of those people burning? I'd like that part of my brain fully removed."

"Ask Mortana," said Orion darkly. "She's the expert at erasing memories."

"She's not Montana," said Shai. "*Mor*tana. Whatever. I've known her since we were seventeen."

"You don't know she was actually seventeen," said Orion. "Do you?"

I was still fighting the nausea. "Well, Orion, if I erased my own memories, I wouldn't remember the spell, would I?" I hoped he felt the sting of that comeback.

Curving sharply, Orion sped onto the highway and headed north. And as he drove, he started connecting his phone to the radio.

"Do you want to let me handle the music so you don't crash?" I asked.

"No." He pushed play, and energetic yodeling blared from the speakers over a deep horn.

Yodelieyoidieohwapidilieayeooo—

I let out a long, slow breath. "Is this it?" I asked. "Is this what Hell is, right now?"

Orion stared straight ahead. "Of *course* you can't appreciate a skilled alphorn solo when you hear one. Philistine."

"Where are we *actually* going?" asked Shai. "Because it looks like we're going to Lawrence. Are we going to be eternally tormented in Lawrence?"

"Hell is not full of torments like you'd imagine," he said. "It's more boring than you'd expect. It's like...Vermont."

My eyebrows rose. "What's hellish about Vermont?"

"Have you ever been to Vermont?" he asked, his voice dripping with disdain.

"Yeah. It's really nice. I visited a maple syrup factory," I said. "Have you?"

"No."

"Okay, it's not hellish. It's beautiful. The leaves are gorgeous. There's amazing cheese and ice cream. Lots of trees. Maple syrup. Like, tons of cows. It's pretty idyllic, honestly. In what way is it supposed to be hellish?"

"There's nothing there," said Shai from the back seat. "The entire state is empty. I mean, apart from the cheese."

"Exactly," said Orion. "I read a history book once outlining everything that happened in the state of Vermont. Do you know what was in it? There were two chapters devoted to a Victorian prize sheep named Gold Drop. One chapter about farmers walking their turkeys to Boston in the eighteenth century. And then there was the greatest event to ever happen in the history of Vermont, which incidentally did not happen in Vermont. Ethan Allen—the great hero of Vermont, conquered Fort Ticonderoga, which is not in Vermont. And when he got there, it was basically empty, apart from two drunk Redcoats."

My brain was scrambling to keep up. "Okay. It sounds peaceful. How is that hell?"

"How is that *not* hell?" he asked, baffled. "Alone, with

nothing but your own memories. Having to live with yourself and everything you've done, with no distractions. That is actual torture, love. You can trust that I would know."

I stared at him, trying to understand. "So that's where we're going? Vermont?"

He shook his head. "No. Not Vermont."

Shai threw her apple core out the window. "Right now, I'm aiding and abetting two criminals. The police could be after me. I'm starting to freak the fuck out. Rowan, you're without a doubt the most anxious person I've ever met. Can you explain why I'm freaking out more than you?"

"Because anxiety is spending all your time imagining terrible situations that might occur," I replied. "Whatever is happening right now isn't a million times different than the apocalyptic scenarios I usually envision. Every night, I go to sleep thinking of the sun exploding tomorrow because the scientists have got the calculations wrong. So this isn't as bad as that."

"I see. And will I be arrested by the mortal police or by the demons?"

"Don't worry about the mortal police," said Orion darkly. "Anyway, I'll need to drop you off soon, Shai. You won't be able to come where we are going. We have to go through the turnpike."

"The Mass Turnpike?" I asked, baffled.

"No. The Veil Turnpike. We're going into the underworld now. It's beyond the veil."

CHAPTER 12—ROWAN

"What does that mean?" I asked. We were zooming along the highway. "The Veil Turnpike?"

"Well, since you don't remember," he muttered. "Before the Great Mortal War, before I was born, the demons lived in the wilderness. Sometimes mortals sought them out, and demons fucked them or got drunk with them. Sometimes demons drank their blood. But really, it was a chance worth taking, given how boring the mortals' lives were."

Overhead, the sky darkened, and a chill rippled through the car. "But some of the Puritans got nervous about it. So they set up rows of sharpened pikes, which had two purposes in those days. One, to create boundaries, and two, to display the severed heads of demons and other enemies. They liked to give warnings that way. Sometimes, at a turnpike, you could pay a toll to get through. They'd open the gate once you paid a price. And where we are going, love, we *will* be paying a price."

An eerie chill rippled over me, and I glanced up at the sky. It was darkening fast, the clouds starting to roil. A storm was rolling in, and it looked strangely unnatural.

Orion glanced over at me. "Open the glove compartment. I have gold and silver coins in there. We'll need them where we're going."

When I did as he asked, the coins practically spilled out onto the floor. I started scooping them up, dropping them into my leather bag. "Gold coins are for paying the toll, I guess?"

"Oh, no. It's not that sort of toll, love."

"What?" I asked. "How is it you can talk so much and clarify so little? It's like the world's shittiest superpower."

Lightning cracked the darkening skies, and Orion cursed under his breath.

"Lord of Chaos," said Shai from the back seat.

"Yes?"

"Weren't you going to let me out first?" she asked. "It feels like something magical is happening now."

Orion shook his head. "They've changed the location."

"So what's going to happen to me?" Shai's voice sounded far way, like she was shouting from a distance.

I turned to look at her. She looked fuzzy, like she was covered in Vaseline.

Fear snaked up my spine. The car seemed to be moving at a terrifying speed, the world outside flitting past in a blur. I was in a car going ninety miles an hour, driven by a complete maniac. I couldn't die in a car crash, but Shai still could.

I turned to look through the windshield again. Rain hammered against the glass. Green blurs rushed around us, and I think we'd veered off the road onto the grass.

"Can you slow down?" I asked.

"No."

Phantoms seemed to rush past the window, mouths agape and eyes wide. A disembodied voice whispered in my ears, "Do you travel with the dark one? Do you come to see the devil himself?"

Inhuman screaming rose around me, sliding through my bones.

Thou wicked creature. Thou wretch! Thou hast undone us body and soul. We shall not suffer a demon to live!

The voice grew louder, a chorus of voices around me.

Dark tree branches grew around the car, surrounding us like clawing fingers. Behind me, Shai was screaming.

Thou hast sacrificed thy kin! Woe unto thee with wickedness in thy veins!

"I did not sacrifice my kin!" I shouted.

The seatbelt tightened around me, choking me. I looked down. It had turned into a rope, one that snaked around my neck. My heart stuttered.

Dizzy, I closed my eyes, trying to master my control of myself. I pulled the leather bag closer, gripping it like it could keep me safe.

In my mind's eye, the image of a beautiful man with bronze skin flickered before me. Black hair, cheekbones sharp as blades, eyes like pale gold…

My heart fluttered at the sight of him.

If thou wilt confess the truth, thou shalt be free. We desire nothing more. Thou shalt not hide thy guilt. Dost thou desire to be Queen of Hell? Confess! A crown just for thee, a wicked star upon thy head...only confession may save thee from eternal flames...

My skin was growing hotter, my pulse racing.

Confess. Confess. Confess!

I opened my eyes again. I could still feel the sensation of a speeding car, but before me was a room made of crude wood and men behind a bench, dressed in black clothes and steep-peaked caps.

The image shimmered away again, but a primal fear shuddered up my nape. Through the blur of the windshield, I saw that Orion was trying to steer the BMW between the trees off the side of the highway. He no longer seemed in control of the car.

Confess!

"I don't know if I'm Mortana!" The confession surprised even me. "I don't remember what happened to Mom. Part of me liked killing the demon hunter. He deserved it. I didn't have any control over this." The confessions were flowing out. "Once, I forgot to pay for a coffee at Starbucks, and I didn't go back. It was a latte. When I'm alone, I say random words like 'corn muffin' and 'oyster crackers' in ridiculous accents. I have a priest fantasy. When I was depressed in high school, I spent a month doing nothing but watching *Love Island*, and I started to speak in an English accent. I had a sex dream about Orion two days ago, but then he turned into a spider, and it was still kind of hot? I pulled the fire alarm once in high school when I had a test—"

My stomach dropped, and I felt suspended in air for a moment before falling.

I slammed onto soft grass, landing hard with an exhale of breath. I stared up, my body buzzing. Overhead, clouds slid past, the lifeless gray of Earth in winter. I stared up at them, dazed and winded. Crows flocked overhead, squawking. I still gripped the leather backpack, clinging to it like a lifeline.

Slowly, I rolled over and looked around to get my bearings. Where was Shai?

The air had the sharp bite of winter, even in early September. An icy gust swept through the trees, strewing fallen leaves in a whirl of bright colors.

I surveyed the world around me. I was lying halfway down a steep, rocky hill that overlooked a valley. To one side, the terrain sloped downward to a dark forest with towering oak trees. On the other side, a hill led up to ancient walls with turrets and towers. Moss grew over stones worn with age. At the bottom of the fortress was a series of dark, misshapen caves. Orion stood near one of them, dusting himself off.

Faintly, I heard screams coming from the caves. Fear prickled over my skin.

Shivering, I got to my feet and slid the backpack over my shoulders. It was about twenty degrees colder here, and my teeth were chattering.

It was then that I realized my clothing had completely changed. I wore a long black dress with an extravagant lace collar and long sleeves. My hair was tucked in a bonnet of some kind. As far as I could tell by the freezing gust of wind rushing over my legs and ass, I was still in the same little underwear I'd been wearing before. But everything else had changed.

This was my goth Puritan look taken to an extreme.

I pulled the backpack off again and searched through it. Everything seemed intact—the money, the water bottles, and the snacks.

Orion ambled closer to me, and I realized his clothing had changed, too. He wore a long, black cloak, and he stalked over with a wicked smile on his lips. "I turned into a spider? I'd love to know what happened in your sex dream before that. Care to elaborate?"

"Oh, good. You heard all that."

He adjusted the front of his dark cloak. "Tell me. Do I look like a priest in this?" A low, velvety laugh. "That's what you like, isn't it? Priests and me?"

"Oh, my God."

"Those were really your worst confessions?" He stepped closer, looking down at me. "You forgot to pay for a *latte*?"

"Am I supposed to feel bad about not being a serial killer?" I looked down the craggy slope. "Where's Shai?"

"She's mortal. She can't cross over. She's in a far safer place than we are. She's still in Massachusetts."

I stroked my fingers over my rough clothes. "So, this is Hell."

"Not quite yet." He nodded at the caves up the hill.

"We will enter the underworld through there. And first, we go through Purgatory."

An agonized scream echoed out of the caves.

"Cool," I said. "Can you give me an idea of what to expect from the torture caves?"

"You can expect demons tormenting you, obviously. But you don't need to worry. It's only mental torture. It's just Belphegor demons fucking with your head. They call it the purification, but don't ask me why. You'll come out physically intact. And as an added silver lining, I can no longer feel the power of the oath here, so I'm not going to murder you. Probably."

Physically intact, but maybe not emotionally. "How long will it take?"

"Oh, four or five days."

"Seriously?"

"Time can pass differently here. But when you are done, you will feel blinding hunger and thirst."

I touched my backpack. "That explains the snacks. And can you tell me what's beyond? What is Hell, exactly?"

"There are many hells. They are places frozen in time, where people play out their same tedious and tragic life events, over and over. We will be like the other mortals there. Once we get out of the caves, our magic won't work. And even if it did, we probably wouldn't want to use it."

"Why?"

"Because this underworld was made from Salem in 1692. They're not fond of magic."

I stared at him, my pulse starting to speed up. Osborne, like its neighbor, Salem, had been caught up in the witch-trials hysteria. In Osborne, thirty-two men and women had hanged, but many more died in the dungeons. "They're stuck in the past," I said, with a dawning sense of horror.

"Demons are drawn to emotions and sin. And that was how the devil came to Salem. The misery in Salem was powerful enough to draw some of the Belphegor demons to Salem, all because of the nonsensical ravings of a bunch of attention-seeking teenagers. The demons drank from tragedy, sadness. They came for the crushing emotional pain, and the Puritans served it up. The demons crawled here, slowly underground. They fed off the misery of typhoid and starvation, and skin lesions in the prisons, from all the lice—"

"That seems very specific."

"Believe it or not, love, I wasn't always the godlike beauty you see before you. Anyway, the Belphegor delighted in the sound of Giles Corey's rasping breaths, the frantic kicking of legs as mortals hanged. And that is how this underworld was created."

I swallowed hard. "Are the people from that time condemned to a miserable afterlife? Some of them were victims."

"Not as many as you might think, love. They were more than happy to watch one another hang."

"Of course. And demons? They're fine. Demons get *off* on evil in a totally normal and morally superior way."

"Right." He cocked his head. "I'll see you in Hell, love."

CHAPTER 13—ROWAN

*H*e turned away, but I grabbed his arm, stopping him. I wanted to delay the next leg of our journey as long as possible because of the whole screaming and torture thing.

"Wait. The Dying God?" I asked quietly. "Who is he?"

"His name is Tammuz, a primordial demon of unparalleled power. He knew my mother."

A shudder danced up my spine. "Have you ever met him?"

"I visited him once. After I escaped. Stop stalling. There is no avoiding Purgatory if we want to break the oath." He turned and started walking, and I reluctantly followed him toward the towering stone walls. "I don't know for certain that he will break the oath," Orion said, "but I do know he's the only one who can." He ran his fingers through his silvery hair. "Tammuz might be one of the oldest demons among us. Maybe that makes him a god. Some say he is Lucifer's dark twin, a god of darkness. For part of every year, he dwells in the underworld. For the rest of the year, he rises from the dead. That's why he's the Dying God."

The wind carried the scent of death, and the sound of screaming rose louder.

The frozen ground was hard beneath my thin leather boots, and my teeth chattered. The wind stung my fingers and cheeks, and a dusting of snow was starting to fall from the heavens.

"Do the people in the underworld know they're dead?" I asked.

"No."

"You said that people there are trapped in their tragedies." My mind flashed with a fragment of a memory from the night Mom was killed, but it was gone again in a moment. One part of me remembered that night. One part of me was still there. "Is that how you feel about your time in the dungeon? Even if you're free, you are always reliving it?"

He turned to look back at me. For a moment, his mask of confidence dropped, and I saw what lay beneath the beautiful surface. Pain, exquisite pain. Then his gaze shuttered again, and he turned away. "Are you trying to be my therapist, Rowan? Because that is a *very* mortal concept, and you're not even qualified."

"No. I'm trying to figure out what made you such a dick."

As we approached the caves, he gave me a half smile. "I tried being nice once. It was boring and overrated."

He'd been saying all along what he was: ruthless,

lethal, lacking in empathy. *I don't hide my flaws or lie about what I am.*

But was that the whole story, or had love twisted him? He'd loved his family, and they were taken from him. Maybe nothing terrified him more than feeling that pain again.

Or maybe, like he'd implied, I was hopelessly naive.

A ray of sunlight escaped the clouds, lighting up the frosted stones around us like a frozen diamond sea. My breath misted around my head. A dusting of snow covered the gray earth before the caves. Near the mouth of a cave, I slipped backward on an icy rock, but with an ungraceful wheel of my arms, I managed to steady myself again.

Orion gave me one last look before he crossed into one of the caves, and I followed after him. Inside, the darkness had a weight, and the silence coiled around us. Wrapped in shadows, I traced my hand against a rocky wall to guide my way until Orion sparked fire in the palm of his hand. Light and shadow writhed over the sand-colored walls, flickering over floor-to-ceiling stalactites and twisted columns of rocks.

Brittle ice cracked beneath my feet. I felt on edge, a sense of unease that increased when an icy wind snuffed out the light in Orion's hand.

Around me, lines of red light carved through the darkness, forming letters from a strange alphabet.

"This is how it begins," said Orion. "You've heard the expression 'the writing on the wall'? Divine judgement, supposedly. *You have been weighed on the scales and found wanting.* Here, in Purgatory, we will be forced to face what we've done. And for a little while, it will be hard to tell what is real from what is a vision."

I took a long breath. "So how will I know when it's over?"

"The writing will disappear." His voice was starting to sound more distant now, echoing from afar. "I will see you on the other side."

I tried to summon fire of my own. After a few moments, though I could feel the rush and spark of magic, the warmth in my palm, I still couldn't see a thing.

Whispers echoed around me, some saying my name, others the name Mortana, drawing the name out in a mocking tone. *Mortaaaaaana*—a chorus of singsong whispers.

"Orion?" My voice sounded muffled, drowned in the sea of whispers. How could whispers be so loud?

Symbols appeared around me, blood-red slashes in the darkness—a language I couldn't read.

From behind me, an agonized scream filled the cavern.

I whirled to see a pale light illuminating a figure on the ground—someone crawling, but there was something very wrong with her. Her arms and legs were bent at strange angles, her head tucked into her chest. I hated the sight of her mangled limbs.

A demon, perhaps? Her skin looked charred, cracked—

I took a step back. "Do you need help?"

But this wasn't real, was it? Orion had warned me—all the demons did was fuck with your head. I closed my eyes, hoping the horrific image would be gone when I opened them again. The creature was still there, crawling closer to me on twisted limbs.

Warm light wavered over the cave walls once more, and a creaking noise filled the cavern.

Do you want to know how you would die? a voice boomed.

"Fuck, no. Do I have a choice?"

I stared at one of the walls, where a hypnotic swaying of shadows moved back and forth, back and forth—until finally, its contours became clear. A woman hung from a noose, her neck crooked at an angle, her hair hanging down, swaying under a bough.

Bright red hair, pale skin. The black dress I wore now.

Sharp terror spread through my gut.

I wasn't in the cave anymore. I was at the bottom of Gallows Hill. A towering elm grew from a rocky ledge halfway up the hill, and I was staring up at my double dangling at the end of a rope. The tree's gnarled boughs were outspread, jagged black lines against a gray sky.

From the foot of the hill, I watched my double's legs twitch and jerk, feet dancing over rocks. The body swayed for hours, the branch creaking under the body's weight. Behind my double, four more bodies hung from nooses—women with purple skin, stiff limbs.

I couldn't move.

They were screaming that I'd sacrificed "my kin," and I wanted to scream, too. How long would this last?

Cold winter air stung my cheeks, smelling of cedar smoke and death. A jeering crowd stood around, screaming curses.

The bough groaned under the weight of my doppelgänger, and her body turned toward me. I caught a glimpse of her eyes—*my* eyes—bulging wide. Her fingers stopped twitching, but her body swayed soundlessly, casting a dark shadow upon the wintry earth.

Dread carved me out.

Why did I feel like this had happened before? It *had* happened before. I'd been here two days, replaying it all.

My breath shallowed. Those bright red letters still gleamed around me. I knew it wasn't real. This was a vision, except…

This *was* going to happen. This was my future.

It had happened before, and it would happen again. We were all trapped, repeating our own tragedies.

The air left my lungs, and I desperately wanted to get out of here.

A curtain of darkness came down over me, sparing me from the horrific vision at last. It was just me in the cave, shaking. But it wasn't over yet. Red slashes still gleamed from the cave walls. The burned woman was still here, shuffling across the cave floor.

I didn't want to see her eyes.

But when she looked up at me, the deep blue pierced

me to the core. I felt something in my hand, cold and metallic.

"I'm so sorry," I muttered, looking down at the set of keys in my palm, so heavy I could hardly hold them.

Guilt ripped me open. I'd done something terrible, and the keys were the evidence. The keys were like a letter branded into my cheek—M for Murderer. I didn't want them anywhere near me.

Flames rose from the woman's body, and she screamed.

The keys filled me with a crushing sense of guilt for sins I could no longer remember. A horror. If I could get these keys away from me, maybe I'd feel better. Maybe I'd be free of the weight of guilt. My tattoo glowed, a golden skeleton key on my arm. Flames rose higher on the woman's body.

I threw the keys into the darkness, and they clattered against stone. I felt a moment's relief, my chest filling with air. The next moment, another set was in my hand, cold and heavy. My hands shook, and I felt as if rocks were pressing on my chest. When I held the keys, I couldn't breathe.

I threw them again, harder this time. The keys returned. I'd never rid myself of their crushing weight—

Again and again, I tried to free myself of them. I kept muttering that I was sorry, that I didn't mean it. I had no idea what I was apologizing for, and I could hardly hear my own voice. Days passed in the same way until at last, the woman disappeared, and the keys along with her.

I breathed in, slowly. Now, the only light in the space was from the vicious writing.

You have been weighed and found wanting.

At last, the letters started to fade into the dark. I let out a long, slow breath as a sense of relief washed over me. I was shaking, and tears rolled down my cheeks.

It was all over now. Fucking hell, that was brutal. And I didn't even understand it.

"Orion?" I whispered. I wiped the tears from my cheeks. I didn't want him to see me cry, but I didn't want to be alone.

That was when the hunger and thirst set in.

I tried to swallow, and my throat burned. Wild hunger ripped through my stomach. My muscles ached, and I thought of an ice-cold chocolate milkshake. I slumped against the wall, delirious.

I'd been standing the whole time, and my legs ached to the bone. Frantic, I slid the backpack into my lap and tore it open. With eager hands, I pulled out one of the bottles of water, thinking as I did that this wouldn't be enough. I'd have to drink Orion's too. But once I'd drained the water, a little more restraint returned.

He'd packed apples, and I ate two of them. These weren't ordinary apples. These apples had grown in the garden of the gods, handpicked by a divine being. Never in the history of food had anything tasted so sweet and succulent, a hint of tart flavor that exploded over my tastebuds.

"Orion?" I asked quietly. I can't say I was eager to have him wake up because I wanted to eat in peace. I mean, I was saving it for him, but it was nice to enjoy this in solitude.

I pulled out a challah roll. It could be moldy by now, but I didn't care. It was still soft and sweet, buttery. The cheese was Comté, the flavor rich and nutty. When I left here, I vowed to eat fondue every day. I would find a French person, thank them for their contribution to the world, and invite them to fondue.

My stomach started to cramp, and I realized I'd eaten too much too quickly. I'd probably started digesting my own organs. I doubled over, clutching my gut. Shoving the rest of the food into the bag, I slung it over my shoulder and started crawling along the cave floor.

"Orion?"

I crawled along on all fours, not unlike the demon I'd seen. After a few minutes, the nausea passed. The water and calories started to hit me, strengthening me a little.

"Orion?"

I forced myself to my feet, steadying myself against the wall.

Once I was upright, I held out my palm and summoned my magic. Warmth tingled down my arm, and fire burst to life in my hand. Light—glorious light.

Never had I been so comforted by fire, but there it was, bathing the caverns in warmth.

But I didn't see anyone else. Maybe he'd already left the caves.

"Orion?" I moved faster through the cavern until at last, pale sunlight pierced the darkness from the mouth of the cave.

Then I saw him at last, slouched against the wall.

Sunlight bathed his enormous body. He was slumped over, a knife in his chest. What the *fuck?* I thought he'd said that the Belphegor demons wouldn't actually hurt us.

Horrified, I rushed forward.

CHAPTER 14—ROWAN

I hurried over to him and knelt. His silver hair hung in front of his eyes, and his coat was open. A knife hilt jutted from his black shirt. I touched his cheek, and his skin felt disturbingly cold.

A tendril of fear coiled through me. He wasn't bleeding. While his eyes were open, they looked lifeless.

For a moment, I was certain he was dead. I pushed his hair back, and fear hollowed me out.

Then the smallest spark flickered in his eyes.

"Orion," I whispered. "I'm going to pull this knife out, okay?"

What the fuck had happened?

On my knees, I grabbed the hilt. If I fucked this up, I could carve out part of his heart—the only way for a demon to die. I didn't know how much leeway I had with this. I wasn't exactly an expert in demon physiology and healthcare.

With one hand on the hilt, I pressed the other on his chest, next to the blade.

Slowly, carefully, I withdrew the blade from his chest. When I pulled out the last bit of the tip, his eyes fluttered. He inhaled, but he still wasn't bleeding. I stared at his heartbreakingly beautiful face, willing him to come alive again.

"Orion!" The panic in my voice echoed off the rocks. His skin felt ice cold, muscles slack. "Orion, wake up."

If he didn't come alive again, then the last thing anyone said to him would be, "I'm trying to figure out what made you such a dick."

His heart had been damaged, so much that it was no longer pumping.

Cold panic crawled over my skin. How did I fix this? I didn't have healing magic.

I froze. That wasn't true, though, was it?

An incubus healed through sex. I'd felt it when I'd nearly died on the way to the City of Thorns, when all I could think about was sex, even if I'd been bleeding all over the place.

I lifted his chin to look him in the eyes. Still alive— just barely. "I'm going to heal you."

His pupils dilated, mouth parting. Already, I could feel the silky warmth of Lilu lust magic caressing us, growing hotter. His eyes darkened, and the look in them was ravenous. I didn't even have to kiss him yet for the magic to start working, to feel electricity crackling between us. All I had to do was want him, which wasn't difficult. And that was good, because he looked very alert now, so I felt less creepy about kissing him.

My heart beating faster now, I slid into his lap. His shadowy eyes searched mine.

I leaned in, pressing my lips against his. Immediately, he seemed to draw strength from me, fingers tightening on my waist. His lips opened, and he kissed me deeply, desperately. Warmth spread through my body, making my pulse race.

As Orion healed, one of his hands moved up my spine, and he threaded his fingers into my hair. I could feel his pulse, his heart coming alive again, beating. He broke away from the kiss and pulled my head back.

His breath had gone shallow, and his hot magic slid over my skin. With a languid swirl of his tongue, he kissed my neck. I laced my fingers in his hair, pulse racing.

"I can't stand you," I said through labored breaths. My pride made me say it, since I knew how he felt about me.

"The feeling is mutual," he whispered against my neck, "but I will die if I don't kiss you."

For one bright moment, it sounded desperately romantic—until I realized he meant it quite literally. He would *actually* die if he didn't kiss me.

Still, I forgot that when he gazed into my eyes again and brushed his thumb over my lower lip. He was looking at me like I was the most exquisite thing he'd ever seen, and I felt my cheeks go warm. He kissed me again, hungrily, his tongue sweeping in. The way he was kissing me, it really didn't *feel* like he found me boring

With one hand, he unbuttoned a few of the buttons on the front of my dress, then pulled away from the kiss, nipping my lower lip in a way that made heat rush to my core. Molten lust pulsed through me, making my thighs clench.

But I wasn't going to let this keep going on—not after what he'd been saying to me. I only needed to heal him, and that was it.

With an iron will, I stopped him from leaning in to kiss me again. He looked at me, his eyes an abyss of midnight.

With my mouth inches from his, I said, "I think we're done. You seem to be feeling better. And as we both confessed earlier, neither of us actually likes each other."

He closed his mouth, jaw clenching. His finger tightened on me. "I could die at any moment. And why deny yourself this pleasure?"

Never in a million years would I admit how much I wanted him. I brushed my hand over the center of his chest, feeling the smooth, completely healed skin beneath his shirt. "What pleasure? I was going through the motions so you didn't die. I was bored."

"Going through the motions? With me? I find that hard to believe."

"Looks like Purgatory left your ego intact." With a supreme act of will, I shifted out of his lap onto the rocky ground. "How did you end up with a knife in your chest?"

For the first time since I'd met Orion, I saw his ever-present self-assurance falter. He was catching his breath. "A snake."

I stood, buttoning my dress again. "A snake stabbed you?"

"No, a snake crawled up my coat, and I stabbed it. Except it was a hallucination." He reached for my backpack and pulled out a bottle of water.

"Orion…are you scared of snakes?"

He unscrewed the top. "The Belphegor demons fuck with your head. That's all."

I supposed I wasn't normally scared of keys. Maybe our tattoos came out to haunt us.

He downed his water quickly, then leaned back against the wall. His eyes had gone pale again. "And what did they show you?" He reached into a bag for his apple. "Did they bring back any memories of condemning all of your kin to death long ago?"

You sacrificed your kin… "It's very thoughtful of you to remind me exactly why I had to stop kissing you."

"Oh? I thought it was because you were bored and going through the motions."

I reached into the bag and pulled out an apple for him. "Have a snack. Maybe you'll become less annoying."

He bit into it, waiting for me to fill him in on what I'd seen.

I sighed. "I saw a demon crawling toward me, and I saw my own death, apparently. Hanging." I stared out of the cave at a forest before us. "It looked like it happened in the clothes I'm wearing now. Can we die here in the underworld?"

"Yes. But I won't let that happen. The demons were just fucking with your head, that's all."

"You won't let it happen?" I slid the backpack on. "Sounds very protective."

He gave me a faint smile. "Long enough to get that secret out of you."

He stood and smoothed the front of his shirt. Buttoning his coat, he walked out of the cave into the blinding winter sun.

I followed him, shielding my eyes from the bright light that glared off the icy earth.

When my eyes adjusted from days of darkness, I took in the scene before me. In the distance, a series of pikes jutted from the earth like bony fingers. On two of the pikes, human heads had been mummified.

And beyond that, a dark forest loomed for miles, the boughs and leaves glittering with ice like diamonds.

The ground felt hard beneath me, frozen.

Orion finished the apple and threw the core aside. "Rowan, why did you heal me? You could have solved all your problems if you'd simply twisted the knife. I'd be dead. There would be no oath to worry about. You could claim the throne for yourself."

"I have empathy, Orion. We've been over this concept before."

He turned to look at me, his expression already bored. "Ah. That died with me long ago in the dungeon." He arched an eyebrow. "But I do suppose I owe you thanks, don't I?"

"You're welcome."

"Did you see anything from your past, Rowan?"

I sucked in a sharp breath, my mind flashing to the horrible memory of those keys. "I saw a set of keys in my vision, and I couldn't get rid of them. It felt like some kind of condemnation." I lifted my arm and pulled up the sleeve. "Do you think it had something to do with this? Something to do with being a demon?"

We passed the gruesome pikes, and the wind toyed with his silver hair. "I'm sure you have things to feel guilty for, Rowan, but being a demon isn't one of them. We are strong, fast, beautiful. We are like gods. And most importantly, we shouldn't feel bad about something we can't control."

"The keys had something to do with Mom." As we moved into the forest, the branches shivered, dusting my black dress with a light fall of snow. "I didn't know my mom as a demon, even if she was one. I knew her as a mortal. She wasn't perfect or godlike or powerful. And she got frustrated and swore and took forever to wake up. But she was the person who used to make me feel better when I was upset. You know how sometimes I get anxious?"

"Oh? I hadn't noticed," he said dryly.

I ignored his sarcasm and went on. "Well, when I was anxious at night and couldn't sleep, she would bring me caramel tea. We would listen to this meditation story on her iPod about a nervous raven, and we would all relax together, me, mom, and the raven named Lenore. Not a goddess, the person who always made me feel better.

And I can't help feeling like I did something to put her in danger."

I thought he was going to make another sarcastic comment or tell me I was rambling, but instead, he fell quiet as we went deeper into the woods. A vault of icy branches arched above us. After a minute, Orion, speaking so quietly that I could hardly hear him, murmured, "My mother used to sing me a lullaby when I had nightmares."

He turned to look at me, and for a moment I, read the acute pain in his eyes.

"Anyway." His expression cleared. "That was a long time ago."

"What do you do when you have nightmares now?"

"Now, love, I *am* the nightmare."

I rolled my eyes, but it wasn't untrue.

CHAPTER 15—ROWAN

We left the forest, and a town common spread out before us, surrounded by zigzagging fences. Cows and goats milled around, languidly chewing on grass. Hills enclosed the common, dotted by timber-frame buildings.

As I took in the shape of the roads wending around the common, I started to recognize its contours.

"I think this is Salem Village. It's now called Danvers." I scanned the horizon, and I pointed to a gently rolling hill. "That's Hathorne Hill, named after one of the witch judges. Later, Danvers State Hospital was built there—a psychiatric institution rife with abuse. It's apartments now. But I always imagined Hathorne's evil spirit haunted the place."

His eyebrows rose. "How did you know all this?"

"Not much else to do in Osborne except learn the sinister history." I glanced at a large black house that overlooked the village—a forlorn-looking building with a gabled roof and a gnarled tree behind it. "This place is creepy as fuck."

"Rowan," whispered Orion, "don't speak too much here. Your accent will stand out."

Fine with me. I'd keep my fun facts to myself, then.

As we approached a dirt road, a man on horseback rode past. He wore a tall, tapered hat and a wide-brimmed white collar. He slowed, staring at us. Suspicious. My heart fluttered a little.

A man was staring at me from several hundred years ago.

It didn't look like Hell, but I knew what kind of dark impulses lurked in the shadows here. Like Orion had so vividly described, neighbors turned on one another. They threw each other in prisons, condemned each other to death.

A cold wind whispered over me as we followed the road past a tall white meetinghouse with mullioned windows and crooked homes. I looked longingly at the warm light, wishing I could be inside somewhere.

A few women passed us, dressed in warm shawls and bonnets and carrying baskets. They eyed us warily.

A river curved to our right, leading to the south.

When we were alone, I whispered, "Where do we find him?"

"In the old Osborne woods," he said quietly.

I swallowed hard. That was where Mom had died.

As we walked, the cold bit into my toes, and my teeth chattered loudly. "We have coins. We might need some warm soup or something on the way."

"I know a place. Keep your voice down."

I was already starving again, and my stomach rumbled.

We walked for what seemed like ages in the cold—past farms, a church, a cemetery with mossy stones and hollow-eyed skulls glaring at us, past horse-drawn carts. A few people nodded and said, "Good morrow."

When we reached a rocky hill, I knew we'd reached Salem Town. There was Gallows Hill, where they'd hanged nineteen people on a rocky ledge. Now, in modern Salem, it overlooked a parking lot behind a pharmacy.

But I was in the grim Salem, where one of the bodies still hung at the end of a rope, a macabre warning to others.

The woman's long gray hair hung down in front of her face, and her feet swayed over the earth. Her body looked stiff and gray, her fingers bony. Lesions covered her skin, probably from her time spent in jail.

My throat tightened at the sight of her, and a miasma of sorrow rose, choking me. Her family must have watched her die.

Never had I wanted to get away from a place so badly.

Orion kept walking along, the wind whipping his silver hair and long cloak. I wasn't sure if he was hurrying away from the corpse or if he simply wasn't interested.

I rubbed my hands together, blowing on them to try to warm them. My breath clouded around me, and I walked faster to keep pace with Orion. The frozen earth chilled my feet through the soles of my thin leather boots.

By the time we reached the famous House of Seven Gables, right on the water, my body was half numb. A stark, gothic mansion loomed over the Atlantic, a deep brown building that was nearly black. The multipaned windows and sharp peaks gave it a witchy appearance, and the iron-gray ocean glittered on the other side of it. Smaller houses surrounded a town square. Here, vendors stood by market stalls, selling vegetables and baked goods.

Just in front of the mansion, a man and a woman hung in the stocks, their heads and arms trapped in wooden openings. It must be an uncomfortable position for them to hold—bent over, necks crooked. A sign at the base of the stocks marked them as *fornicators*.

Mud clumped their hair and coated their hands.

"Whore!" someone shouted from a window.

The woman winced like she'd been hit with a rock.

Of course, the Jack Corwins of this world had always existed, hadn't they?

I tried not to stare at them, but the woman glanced at me from under a curtain of filthy hair, her face etched with misery.

Could fornication be worth this punishment? Depended on the guy, I supposed.

As we crossed behind them, I grimaced at the sight of their bare backs, covered in dried and frozen blood where they'd been whipped. They were naked from the waist down, blood dried in stripes on their skin.

Orion turned to me, looking bored. "We can eat there."

"What?" The comment was jarring, given the gruesome scene before us. "Orion," I whispered, "does this stuff not bother you?"

He glanced at the flogged couple like he'd just realized they were there. "I thought you were hungry. Follow me."

He led me to a wooden building. A gray sign above the door was marked with a picture of a cauldron. As soon as we entered, the smell of food made my mouth water. I surveyed a hall of dark wood, with wooden beams that crossed the ceiling. A large iron pot bubbled on the hearth, and a few people sat at wooden tables sipping beer. Others gathered at a wooden bar in the center of the room. The warmth was *glorious*.

Silence fell over the tavern, and everyone turned to look at us—men, women, children. I think even the cat on the bar turned to stare. But the cozy atmosphere drew me in, with firelight that danced back and forth over the room and steam rising from the hearth. After a few breaths, everyone turned back to their food and drinks.

Orion crossed to a table by the window. Steam clouded the glass, and I wiped my hand across it to peer outside. From here, we had a view of the town square. It was hard not to stare at the misery of two people in the stocks, but that was the point, wasn't it? Control people by making the punishments public. Extra humiliating, and it also kept everyone else in line. No one wanted to be in their situation.

It took me a moment to realize that Orion was

speaking to someone else, and I snapped out of my dark daydream to see a young woman standing at our table. Her hair was covered with a white cap, and she stared at Orion with wide blue eyes. "And why would you be going to Osborne, Goodman Ashur? I never set foot in the place." She fluttered her eyelashes. "Osborne is full of evil magic and fornicators. The demon city is there, and I pray that they stay inside. But they say a devil lurks in those woods. They say he escaped in the Great War, that the binding spells do not touch him. You should not go near that place, I pray you, lest you die."

Goodman Ashur?

"It sounds terrible," said Orion with only the *slightest* hint of sarcasm. I could only hope this woman wouldn't notice. "*Fornicators?* So vile a thing."

She leaned in, whispering. "Detestable beasts. When you arrive in Osborne, tell them Goody Putnam herself said the devil has made his home in their woods because of their wickedness. Tell them I said their dark forest turns people into animals. Naked, dripping with blood. The women rut with the Shadow Man in the woods like foul beasts, on their hands and knees, shrieking in bestial pleasure." She looked absolutely delighted, her eyes dancing, cheeks pink. "They have made a diabolical covenant with him. I have seen it with my own eyes."

I wanted to say, "I thought you never went to Osborne," but I'd been told to keep my mouth shut.

If what she said was true and women were running around naked, rutting in the woods with a demon, maybe that explained why the Dying God hung around here half the year. Whoever he was, he was probably more fun than the dour-looking mortal men slurping soup in this tavern. No wonder he had a following. And no wonder Goody Putnam had gone out looking for him.

Orion straightened, and his pale eyes glinted in the warm candlelight. "Woe to him that coveteth an evil man. We seek to *expel* the devil from these good towns. It is our sacred mission, dangerous as it may be. It is my most fervent wish to drive this beast into hellfire and burn his devil's book so that no more innocent women may be corrupted by his malevolence."

"Of course." Her cheeks reddened, and she smiled at him. "You are a goodly demon hunter." She continued to stare at him, enraptured. "Aye, the Malleus Daemoniorum. We have heard that you would come to purify these shores. We have been waiting for you." She leaned in closer. "We are honored to have a man like yourself here to protect us, courageous and strong as you are."

You've *got* to be kidding me. Even here, women flirt with him?

Orion steepled his fingers. "And this devil. You think he's still in the Osborne woods?"

"Oh, aye. 'Tis a cursed forest. I seen him there a few times by myself, surrounded by naked women writhing in a shameful dance. Wild with lust of the flesh. The forest makes them feel evil things. Do you know, the devil looked at me for one moment, and he could sense the goodliness within me? It angered him. He did howl like a wild beast to drive me away into the night." Her hand strayed down her chest, her face glowing with the memory.

It *kind* of sounded like Goody Putnam had been wandering around the sex forest, hoping for a rut with the devil, but she was too weird, even for him.

"Most impressive, Goody Putnam," said Orion, his face deadly serious. "You are a blessed woman."

She giggled. "How tall are you? I have never seen a man so tall. You are taller than a stallion."

I opened my mouth to ask about food, but Orion touched my arm. "My wife has taken a vow of silence to repent for her sins."

I suppose I had to be his wife here, or I could end up clapped in the stocks like the unfortunate couple outside.

Wait a minute—*sins*?

The woman turned to me for the first time. "Oh, sins?" She frowned. "There is something familiar about her wanton face. Perhaps a terrible dream. But what sins? She must confess in public."

I could only shrug.

The faintest of smiles curled the corner of Orion's lips. "To atone for her wicked temptations, her corrupted lust of the flesh that can never be satisfied. But she is repenting now."

"Oh." A look of disgust crossed the woman's face. "Aye, I can see it in her eyes." She shuddered dramatically. "Keep her away from that forest."

I kicked Orion under the table.

"And this devil," Orion went on. "Where in the forest

did you see him, when you were out at night so carefully avoiding temptation?"

"Up on the rocky hilltop, under the moonlight." I could see the delight in her eyes. "I'll bring you the lobster, then, so you have sustenance for your fight against darkness." She shot me a sharp look, judgment burning in her eyes.

Don't look at me like that, Goody Putnam. I know what you were doing in those woods.

CHAPTER 16—ROWAN

*B*ecause Goody Putnam clearly had the hots for Orion, she'd let us take two pewter flagons of fruity, hot beer with us, which she called "chowder," fresh from the cauldron. Her jealousy had been palpable. I wouldn't be surprised if she found herself wandering into the evil woods later to help *Goodman Ashur*.

She might have been annoying, but the chowder was starting to make me appreciate her. Steam from the beer warmed my cheeks as we walked toward Osborne, and the hot metal kept my fingers warm.

A winding road led past tottering buildings from Salem to Osborne as we walked west, away from the sea. We passed gently rolling farmland. Cows stood in the cold fields, chewing grass, and wisps of steam rose from their bodies into the frigid air. Farmhouses were painted in subdued colors—pale yellow, cream, and deep brown.

A dirt road threaded between them. Leaves trembled from boughs, bright orange like flickering flames.

"Orion, what's next for you?" I asked quietly when no one was around. "After you kill Cambriel and take over the city, what do you plan to do with your power? You haven't told me."

"I think I'll start with reclaiming everything they took from us."

I raised my eyebrows. "When you're done, will there be anyone left in the City of Thorns to rule over?"

"Let's assume some of them are smart enough not to get in my way."

As we walked further into town, the buildings became more crowded. Dark-wood houses leaned over the road, and I could no longer see the shore. By now, the sky was darkening over the sea, streaked with periwinkle and crimson.

From here, we could see the City of Thorns in the distance. I'd nearly forgotten it would be here, too, but there it was, crowning Osborne's tallest hill, its golden walls shrouded in mist.

I stared at it. Was a little Orion in there, imprisoned in their dungeons? Could he be stopped from becoming the damaged person he was now?

I grabbed his arm and nodded to the east. "What happens if you go in there?"

He leaned in close, his lips near my ear. "I tried it. It doesn't work. You can't get past the walls. And the Dying God tells me all tragedies are replayed here. They cannot be stopped."

I nodded, and we started walking again, closing in on the dark forest.

On the street where I'd lived—now Walcott Street, with the Dollar Store and Dunkin'— the buildings had grown more sparse. This was Witchcraft Point.

Gallows Hill, that craggy slope, rose up to our left. There on the ledge, beneath the jagged bough of an elm, dangled the bodies of four women.

The bough creaked and groaned beneath their weight, the sound carrying on the wind like a phantom,

That was where I'd been hanged in the vision. A little tendril of horror wound through me. From here, I couldn't see their faces, but I could see that their hair hadn't turned gray. They were young, like me. In a man's world like this, you could get in trouble for being old and ugly and past your prime. Or you could get in trouble for being young and tempting. Women like that made a man sin. And that, of course, was your fault, too.

I glanced at the four corpses as we went by, their bodies stiff and gray.

I stole a quick glance at Orion. When power was in the wrong hands, it was dangerous as hell. No way should Orion have absolute power over a kingdom. He was damaged, broken, obsessed with revenge. He would be an absolute nightmare. Executions, purges, torture— probably a slow and painful death for me, if he still thought I was Mortana.

"Why do I feel like you're scheming something?" Orion purred in a velvety tone.

I blinked innocently. "Because you're delusional and deeply paranoid?"

A quiet, joyless laugh escaped him, and his pale eyes were luminous in the dusk. "Scheming and evading. How very Mortana of you."

The wind toyed with my red hair. Was it possible that Mortana was just looking out for herself when she'd sold everyone out, because she had to?

We headed north into the forest. I thought my old house was right around here, and I wished I could travel to a different time.

The wind howled through the trees ahead, rustling the leaves as we approached the edge of the woods. In here, snow and ice encrusted many of the trees, and waxy orange mushrooms ringed some of the trunks.

Take the ring,
fell the king.
The city yet will thrive.

It was starting to feel like an instruction—one that my parents had left behind for *me*. Not for someone like Orion.

The question was, how could I possibly defeat him?

Clearly, he was more adept at killing than I was, and I'd made an oath to tell him about Cambriel's ring.

As we moved through the trees, the sun dipped lower, staining the treetops blood-red. Under the forest's canopy, shadows spread out, and a crow screeched, piercing the air.

In the forest, the air smelled of moss and soil. Snow fell heavier than before.

I felt the cold caress of something powerful, electrifying in these woods. A magic that drew me inexorably closer, beckoning me. I wanted to go deeper into the forest, to taste danger.

The distant howling of a wolf raised goosebumps on my skin.

We moved on through the trees, our footfalls crunching over frosty leaves. Maples and hickories grew tall around us.

Orion's eyes beamed from the shadows, luminous and demonic. "Rowan, do I sense fear? Are you afraid of the woods?"

"Maybe not fear. Sadness." I blew out a cloud of breath, my mind flashing with the worst night of my life, racing through the trees to get away from my mom's killer. With most people, this is where I would lie to them. No one *really* wanted to hear about something that terrible. But with Orion? The darkness didn't scare him. "My mom burned to death in these woods."

He stopped walking, his gaze locked on mine. "And what is it that makes you scared?"

I blew out another cloud of breath, thinking about his question. "Memories. I'm afraid I'll remember what happened that night."

A line formed between his eyebrows. "Are you worried it was you?"

I felt the breath leave my lungs. "No. But there are still things I can't remember."

"You feel guilty for something."

It was a statement of fact, and it was a hundred

percent correct. I wasn't sure I wanted to admit it. "I have no idea what for."

"Maybe because you lived, and she didn't. And all you will see are reasons why you didn't deserve to live."

'Thanks," I said sharply.

"Not because they're the truth, because that's what happens when you're the one to survive. It feels like the gods made the wrong choice. When someone is hunting you down, like they did you and your mother—when someone more powerful than you tries to kill you—you make split-second decisions. And sometimes, those decisions are at the expense of someone else. If someone is starving to death, maybe they don't share all their food. When people are freezing, maybe they take a coat from a dying person. And when you were running from a killer in the woods, maybe you made the right decision, and your mom didn't. Maybe you just kept going, and that's how you survived. Maybe that's why you don't feel you deserve it."

A stream of moonlight pierced the canopy. When Orion looked at me, I could read a deep, lacerating sorrow in his eyes. "Demons and mortals alike have a very strong instinct of self-preservation. It's how we are made. People are selfish when death is staring us in the face. There's no point pretending otherwise, and there's no point feeling bad about it."

Maybe he was right. "Okay."

"Trust me, love," he said quietly. "If you try to fight your true nature, you will lose, and you will break in the struggle. Accept what you are, and it will be less painful."

A frozen wind rushed over me. What, exactly, *was* my true nature? Maybe our natures changed over time, because I wasn't the same girl I'd been a few months ago.

The forest air kissing my skin felt warmer now. I felt lighter, too. Maybe what Orion had said resonated with me.

Mist twined between the trees, then seemed to snake and writhe around Orion. Moonlight tinged the fog with silver. I had no idea why it would get warmer at night, but I didn't hate it.

The air smelled thick with moss and salt, earthy and luxurious. I inhaled, my muscles relaxing.

I glanced at Orion. As always, he moved with languid, catlike ease. When he caught me looking at him, he gave me a faint smile. It was the first time I noticed he had a little dimple in his cheek, and I felt a strange flush of heat. Masculine power rolled off him, stroking my skin and making my heart race.

Catching my breath, I pulled my gaze away from him, walking faster. He was an incubus, and I was falling under his spell again. That was all that was. I gripped the straps of my backpack as I hurried along.

Remember, Rowan, he wants to get away from you. He can't stand you.

With that unpleasant thought, I sped up to get out of range of his incubus magic. We needed to get this journey over with and get out of each other's lives.

We couldn't be too far from Tammuz because I could hear the sound of the ocean rhythmically crashing against the shores. My body moved to the sound, swaying. Distantly, I heard the beating of a drum, and my heart pounded to its seductive rhythm.

It wasn't just Orion's words. Something was happening to me.

CHAPTER 17—ORION

Goody Putnam was bloody right about one thing: these woods did inspire a wicked lust. And because I was with Rowan, the music of the forest came alive—the rustling of leaves, the songs of owls and mockingbirds. Icicles shone with unearthly light.

And all I could think about was fucking her up against a tree.

She looked at me, and I recognized a flicker of sadness in her dark eyes. My heart clenched.

Part of me wanted to kiss her right here. She might *not* be the evil Mortana I'd come to know. She couldn't be.

But nothing was more dangerous than hope. Mortana had taught me that a long time ago. It was her greatest lesson to me.

Sometimes, she would tell Ashur and me that in a few weeks, we'd be set free. I remember the indescribable joy, thinking of what we'd do, of the sunlight on our faces. We'd count the days, looking through the cracks in the wall to see when the sun rose.

And when the few weeks were up, she'd pout and say, "Sorry, darling. I can't bear to lose you."

It happened again and again before I'd finally learned. I was her rival for the throne, and she delighted in seeing me crushed completely.

I think that was what killed Ashur at last, the disappointment of feeling so close to freedom, then having it destroyed. After one of Mortana's visits, he'd stopped eating.

When I looked at Rowan, I felt those embers heating again. *Maybe she was different...*

But I'd learned my lesson already. At the last moment, she'd probably find some way to deceive me, to leave me without the secret I craved. I must remember that. More likely than not, she would extinguish any flame of hope I had left.

"Do you feel that?" Rowan asked. "The magic of the Dying God is all around us."

She was right. Here, Tammuz's magic flowed strong. Whatever it was, a primal magic enchanted every bough, every rock, and the mossy carpet beneath our feet.

Rowan walked ahead of me, shivering, which against all reason made me want to pull her close. I had a coat on, and she did not. But I never felt the cold anymore. The dungeons hadn't been heated, and in January and February, ice had slicked the walls and the cold stone floor. For a hundred and fifty years, I didn't have a blanket. I'd learned to sleep on the ice.

For a moment, I considered giving her my coat, but that would be insane. If she *was* Mortana, I would have to kill her. And how was I supposed to do that if I could hardly manage watching her teeth chatter?

In the distance, I glimpsed a little stone cottage between the trees, and I felt an overwhelming urge to take her there and warm her up by a fire.

I had one purpose in this world, and it was not to make my worst enemy comfortable. What she'd done to my mother and Ashur and all the rest—that should have been enough to extinguish the smoldering fire of my lust.

Her hips swayed as she walked, inviting me closer. Even in her ridiculous woolen dress, she was making me hard. It was her succubus scent, like deliciously ripe fruit, and the fact that I knew exactly how glorious she looked naked. Alabaster skin, pink nipples—

Bloody hell. This would be a lot easier without *that* memory burned into my mind—Rowan's hips in the air and her body aching for mine.

I tightened my fingers into fists. I could tell myself she was my enemy, my rival, but my body had other designs. My body had decided she was mine, and that we belonged together.

Since I lacked self-restraint, I would have to rely on the groundwork I'd laid earlier: brutally insulting her. If I couldn't keep myself from her, I hoped that would keep *her* from *me*.

I can finally rid myself of your irritating presence.

It was the one sensible thing I'd done since she'd come back.

My gaze slowly raked down her back to her narrow waist. My hunger for her was unbearable, my incubus side starved for her touch, for the warmth she inspired in me.

She looked back at me, a question in her eyes. From all appearances, she didn't understand this world anymore, which made it harder to remind myself who she was.

As the sea wind toyed with her red hair, she seemed entranced with me. The magic of the forest was affecting both of us.

My gaze lingered over her heartbreakingly beautiful face, her full lips.

"These woods are enchanted," she murmured. "I'm starting to feel…a bit more like a demon."

A bit more like a succubus.

I wanted to maintain my mask of boredom and say something insulting, but instead, I moved closer. She pressed her hand against my chest. To keep me at a distance, perhaps, but her touch made my heart pound.

I could hear her heart beating in time with mine, hear the shallowing of her breath.

"There's a cottage." I nodded up ahead. "You could get warm there before we move on."

Mortana. She was Mortana.

She held my gaze steadily, breath clouding around her face. Something mischievous glinted in her eyes. "Do you actually find me tedious? When we first met, you told me that you didn't lie about what you were, and that's what made humans different from demons, but I'm not convinced you were telling the truth." Her eyebrows drew together, and a pink flush rose over her cheeks. "Why did you really let me live?"

Of course, she was absolutely fucking right, and she fascinated me more than anyone. I wasn't about to admit it, though, since it was the only thing saving me from complete self-destruction.

"If you think I like you, it's my incubus charm." I slid my hands into the pockets of my coat. "Everything I said stands. You're nothing but a beautiful irritant." I forced the words out, though it felt like I was hearing them from a distance, ridiculous words that had no meaning.

She cocked her head. "You did say beautiful, though."

Had I?

"But that's not really good enough. If you genuinely think I'm nothing more than an irritant and have no respect for me at all, then you have terrible taste. That makes you not good enough, I'm afraid. You've been weighed on the scales and found wanting. You know, Orion? Maybe a mortal man could truly appreciate me."

She turned away, and I felt it like a physical pain, claws plunging into my chest. Insane, irrational jealousy surged through my veins, even though I wasn't even sure who I was jealous of. A mortal?

My demon side took hold, darkness spilling out around me. My body was taking over my mind.

I prowled after her. I *had* to have her because she was mine.

Blood pumping hot in my veins, I grabbed her arm and spun her around to face me. Her eyes darkened, and her lip curled back, exposing her fangs. *There* was the beautiful demonic side of her, the ferocious succubus. She let out a hiss.

What was I doing?

"I don't find you boring at all," I admitted. "I hate you for what you did. But because I'm certain that I am cursed, I can't stop thinking about what it would feel like to have your legs wrapped around me and your mouth pressed to mine. And I can never, *ever* stop thinking about you."

With a wicked smile, she stroked her hand down my chest. "It's too bad you hate me, then, isn't it?" A little shrug of her shoulders. "I can easily find someone who doesn't. Didn't Goody Putnam imply the Dying God was beautiful?"

Aggression unfurled inside me, and I pressed her against an oak tree, boxing her in with my palms on the rough bark. I wanted to fuck her until she forgot he existed.

She stared up at me, her eyes wide. "Oh, dear. Are you jealous?"

She was toying with me, of course.

"I'm going inside. You'll freeze if you stay out here." I started walking, and I heard her follow me. We were close to the cottage now, a crooked little place made of stone and covered in snowy ivy.

"Why do you care if I'm freezing?" she asked. "Since you hate me."

She could see right through me, which was annoying. "I need to make sure you don't freeze to death before you tell me how to kill Cambriel."

This was a bad idea, but I was already pushing through the door into the little cabin. It didn't look like anyone had been here in a while, but it had the potential to be cozy. A fireplace in the hearth stood empty, and I crossed over to it. A pile of logs stood next to the fireplace, and I started sliding them in, one by one, arranging kindling on the bottom. A curled metal fire-striker lay on the floor, along with paper and flint. Vaguely, I remembered these little tools from my childhood, and I struck the metal against the flint until it sparked, igniting the paper. I dropped the flaming paper onto the logs and watched the flames spread.

It gave me a chance to clear my head and remind myself not to let this woman give me hope again. I pushed one of the logs with an iron poker, watching the flames rise. There was something deeply satisfying about lighting a fire in the dead of winter.

With the fire burning, I surveyed the rest of the cottage, a single room with a little wooden stairwell leading to a loft. A low bench sat across from the fireplace, and a black bearskin rug covered the floor. Mentally, I'd stabilized myself once more.

But when I looked up at Rowan, washed in the golden light of the flames, I could hardly think straight.

The magic of the forest had muddled my thoughts, I told myself, reviewing all the reasons I shouldn't touch her.

I rose from a crouch, trying to read something in her eyes. Was she going to attempt to break my spirit again?

I looked down at her, fighting the urge to kiss her.

Her eyebrows climbed. "So why lie to me? Why tell me that I bore you?"

"To keep you away from me, because I don't trust myself to resist you." *Fuck.* I leaned down, breathing in her scent. Her neck arched, inviting me. "The thing is, Rowan. I know how much you want me, too. It's part of being an incubus. I can practically taste your arousal. You drive me mad, but I know I do the same to you."

Her cheek brushed against mine, the soft feel of her skin driving me wild. I pulled back, staring into her eyes, drunk on her beauty.

Moonlight gleamed off her dark irises. "Even if that were the case, incubus, what are you going to do about it?"

"I plan to ruin you with a kiss."

The little smile on her lips was a dare, an invitation. I sensed her need, desire rippling from her body. Her allure was a command I had to obey.

She dropped her backpack on the floor. "What exactly does that mean, *ruin me with a kiss*?"

I trailed a finger over her throat, watching her body react. "I'm the last incubus in the world. After me, no one else could ever compare. You'll be ruined forever, love."

CHAPTER 18—ROWAN

*D*amn it.
    I moved nearer, inviting his touch.

He knew exactly how to turn me on, with a look, with that intense expression, with a murmur of his deep, caressing voice. Sliding his hands around me, he pulled me closer.

I had a sudden impulse to be at his level and stepped onto the low bench, putting myself at his height. He gave me a knowing smile, a lock of silver hair falling before his eyes.

"Ruin me?" I tried to play it cool, but my voice sounded husky. I pushed him, which was childish, but this forest had made me irrational. "The arrogance is truly breathtaking. I really should have listened the first time you told me what a terrible person you are."

The sultry look in his eyes made my pulse race as his gaze swept slowly down my body. Every inch of my skin heated with desire, aching for his touch.

I needed to put an end to this. Of *course* nothing could happen between us. After all, I needed to take the crown from him. He was my rival. And maybe he really *would* ruin me.

"I think you're a terrible person," I said.

"We have that in common," he murmured.

"You don't deserve to be king." I reached for the collar of his coat, pulling it down over his shoulders with a rough tug. The garment dropped to the bearskin rug. "And you don't deserve these luxurious clothes."

"Are you trying to strip me, love? Go on, then. You're right. I don't deserve to be king." A sensual curve tugged at the corner of his lips. His mouth was an inch from mine now, his expression smoldering. "And yet, I'm going to be king anyway, and there's fuck all you can do about it."

Under his coat, he wore a buttoned shirt—ripped a little by the knife blade. I started popping the buttons open, one at a time. "You don't deserve the crown. You should still be living in filth in your dungeon." I pulled his shirt off and stared at perfection. His golden body practically glowed in the firelight. My gaze slid over his thickly corded arms, his divine abs.

"I hate you," I whispered. I didn't hate him, but I wanted to make it even, since he'd said the same to me several times.

This place had intensified my emotions beyond all reason. Annoyance became hatred. And attraction? That became uncontrollable sexual need.

"You think I should be in the dungeon still?" His voice was a seductive murmur, mouth hovering near mine. "I think you should be stripped naked and begging me to let you come. I think I'm going to make you call me your king, whether you want to or not."

"Absolutely not."

For a moment, I thought he was going to kiss me. Instead, with a low growl, he grabbed the front of my dress at the collar and ripped it, pulling it down to my waist. He kept tearing at it until I was clad in nothing but a pair of small midnight blue underwear.

I caught my breath, and my nipples went rock hard. Torn between lust and anger, I reached out and stroked the side of his face. "If you ask me, you should still be in the dungeon."

His expression darkened. "Is that right? Perhaps it's time I taught you a lesson. Is that what you're asking for?"

In a graceful movement, he sat down on the bench and pulled me into his lap. The next thing I knew, I was facedown, bent over his knees. Quite undignified.

"What are you doing?" I sounded irritated, but the truth was, I could have moved if I'd wanted to.

"Teaching you a lesson, love." His hand moved slowly down my spine, and he stroked the back of my underwear, his fingers grazing between my thighs. "After all those years of you torturing me, I think it's time we switched roles. And do you know what?" His voice was thick with seduction, and he cupped me between my legs. "As king, I really should claim what I want to be mine."

Searing need pulsed through my body, between my thighs. I could have reminded him that wasn't me, but—again—I didn't want to.

When he pulled down my underwear sharply, my breath hitched. I was practically shaking with need, my body begging to be touched by him. His left hand gripped me by the hair, holding me in place. As he slid my panties down my thighs, I became turned on beyond all reason. My lust was spiraling out of control. All I could think about was how badly I needed him inside me.

He brought his hand down hard on my ass, a momentary sting that was soon replaced by a wave of pleasure. I shifted my hips against him, wanting *more*, and he delivered as I arched my hips to meet his hand. Another stinging smack on my ass—and another—sent shivers of insatiable need through my body until I could no longer stand it.

"You know," he purred, still gripping my hair, "I have always wanted to see you completely helpless before me." He traced his fingertips over me, touching me where I was wet. He slid one finger inside me, and I clenched around him with a moan.

"I can feel how much you want me," he whispered. "But I'm going to need to hear you say it. Say that I'm your king."

I was going to lose my mind. I was getting close to

orgasm. With the ache rising in my core, I was ready to do anything he wanted, say anything he wanted—

He pulled his fingers away from me again, and I gasped.

I had no response, just a wild desperation for more contact, more friction. Because he was right, I was completely at his mercy right now.

I wasn't going to let him drag out this torture any longer. Pushing myself out of his lap, I let my underwear drop to the floor.

He stared at me in awe as I stepped between his legs, unbuttoned his pants, and tugged them down.

"Come here," he said.

I climbed onto his lap, straddling him. He leaned into me, kissing me. His tongue swept in, and he stroked a hand down my body, over my ribs, my waist.

He froze and pulled away from the kiss, his gaze sliding down my naked body. Gently, he traced the scar on my side. "What happened?"

I had no interest in talking about the scar right now. It seemed an unfortunate distraction. "The demon hunters."

A quiet, possessive growl rose from his chest. "If you weren't within the city walls when it happened, you weren't able to heal completely. They tried to kill you when you were most vulnerable."

The warmth of the fire heated my back. "Forget it. That's the last thing I want to think about."

Orion rose and scooped me up, then lay me down on the rug. The fur tickled my skin.

Grabbing my wrists with one hand, he pinned them above my head on the bearskin. Usually so controlled, his dark expression was now wild. In fact, he looked like he was about to fuck me senseless, which was exactly what I wanted.

"Orion," I whispered, "I want you to know that I still think you're the absolute worst."

"That's one thing we agree on." He moved between my thighs and lowered his head to my breast, taking one nipple in his mouth. I moaned, my hips thrusting forward against him. A raw groan escaped his lips, and he worked his mouth over my peaked breast. The ache in my core had become insatiable.

"Open your eyes and look at me, love," he purred. "I want to see how much you want me."

I did as he asked. There was always something instantly hot about the way he stared at me. "Does it make you feel powerful?" My lips curled into a little smile. "In control?"

A soft laugh. "Yes."

But from the wild look in his eyes, I could see he was ready to lose control, too. As well-endowed as he was, it was impossible to ignore how turned on he was.

With a sudden burst of strength, I ripped my wrists from his grasp and reached for his underwear, pulling it down.

I stared for a moment at his intimidating length, wondering if this was an incubus trait. I reached down to touch it, to stroke it. He groaned, the air heating around him, and uttered a demonic curse. He gripped my wrists again, pinning me down to the floor. Possessive.

For a moment, he was pressed against my wet heat, his mouth hovering above mine. Desire coiled tightly in me, and I shifted my hips, moving against him.

"Are you going to admit I'm your queen?"

"No, love, because you're my worst enemy," he whispered, "but this I will admit. I can't stop thinking about you, and I never will."

Slowly, he slid into me, one inch at a time, his size nearly overwhelming me. "Tell me how much you want me," he said, and I could hear the strain in his voice. He was using everything in himself to maintain control.

"I think you know, Orion."

He slid inside me as far as he could go. He paused, searching my eyes to see how I felt, and I wanted him to stop holding back.

He pressed his lips against mine, delivering a kiss that would surely ruin me, as promised. His tongue slid against mine in a sensual caress. Slowly, he moved his hips back, then he thrust into me again.

Never in my life had I imagined anything could feel this amazing. I tightened my thighs around him.

He pulled away from the kiss, his gaze searching mine again. "You don't know how many times I have thought of this." His voice sounded raw, ragged, and his mouth lowered near my throat.

He was moving a little faster now, and he kissed me again—harder, more desperately, his tongue sweeping against mine as he fucked me.

As he thrust into me, intense pleasure made me moan into his mouth, my body coiling tighter with a need for release. He was moving faster now, with an animalistic ferocity, as if he were claiming me.

I moaned his name, throwing my head back against the rug, my breasts sliding against his chest.

I would have said anything in that moment, but I couldn't remember what it was he'd wanted me to say. My entire world had narrowed to the feel of him inside me, giving me the intense pleasure I'd craved for so long.

As my climax built, I breathed his name, over and over.. My climax ripped out of me, my body tightening around him.

"Rowan." He said my name with reverence, and then, with a shudder, he groaned against my neck as his fingers clenched under my ass. Orion wrapped his arm around me, his head resting against my neck. By the slump of his shoulders, he looked defeated. I touched his cheek.

Shuddering with the aftershocks, I caught my breath. His muscles had relaxed, and he held my gaze.

I stroked his muscled back. "I may have just ruined my life, but it was worth it."

I wanted him to kiss me again, but this wasn't love, was it? He'd made that perfectly clear.

He had the posture of a man who'd lost a battle. So who had actually been ruined here? I wasn't so sure it was me.

He pushed himself up on his elbows, staring into my

eyes again. For the first time, he looked strangely innocent. Vulnerable, maybe.

"Orion?" I said, remembering my ripped dress. "I'm going to need your coat for the rest of the trip."

CHAPTER 19—ROWAN

*W*e walked on snow-covered paths, the forest's magic still pulsing through the air. It swirled around inside my skull like a potion. I shivered in Orion's coat, nearly naked under the scratchy wool.

I hoped we found this Dying God before I got frostbite in very unfortunate places. The coat didn't fit me at all, and the pressure of the backpack kept popping a button open. As the bottom of the coat dragged over the forest floor, snow accumulated on the hem.

I tried to picture myself in the oversized wool garment and was pretty sure I looked like a nineteenth-century Russian clown.

Orion walked by my side, his hands in the pockets of his cloak. Now he looked completely relaxed, and he gave me a mischievous glance. "Sorry about the dress."

"Was tearing it really necessary?"

"Absolutely."

Did I regret what we'd just done? Given the way my body still felt, humming and electrified, I couldn't say that I did. Besides, there was no point in regretting something you couldn't control. Might as well bemoan the need to breathe. What was the point? Once he'd said he was going to ruin me with a kiss, I'd needed him like I needed oxygen.

There was no choice—my desire for him was like a command from a god.

I did regret the loss of the dress, though, because the biting wintry air sneaked into the gaps in the coat, stinging my bare skin, and the bottom of the coat had grown damp with the snow.

When an unnatural, silvery glow illuminated the trees, my mood improved. We were close, surely. The moonlight gleamed upward, beaming from the forest floor to the skies.

I tugged the coat tighter around me, wondering how much weirder things could get. I was about to meet a demon god wearing a wool tent with buttons and my tits ready to pop out.

"He's here," Orion said with a quiet reverence. He'd never seemed sure if the gods were real, and I wondered if he actually believed deep down.

From the corners of my eyes, lights flickered. I turned my head and caught glimpses of letters—not an alphabet I recognized. Cuneiform, maybe. Around me, writing formed, bright, vicious lines of light that looked like a knife had hacked through the darkness, revealing starlight behind it.

I touched Orion's arm. "What's all this?"

"Sumerian," he whispered. "Once, demons were worshipped as gods in the ancient world. Tammuz is one of the oldest among us. He lived as a god."

Whispers fluttered around me, but I couldn't make out the words at first. Then, I heard it—*Chaos. Chaos. Chaos.*

Goosebumps rose on my arms. Lord of Chaos—I thought that was Orion's thing...

"Do you hear that?" I whispered.

He lifted his finger to his lips. The light around us silvered his face.

He'd gone completely still, and after another minute, he finally spoke. "I'm going to summon him now."

Orion began speaking quietly in a rhythmic, percussive language. The dark and beautiful phonemes seemed to send me into a trance.

The glowing cuneiform symbols flickered away, and shadows stole the light in the forest. A low rumbling sound trembled over the forest floor, as if the earth were pregnant with thunder. Fear slid through my bones.

Stars glittered between naked boughs, illuminating the demon god.

Ice and snow encrusted the trees in the grove, gleaming with cold light like wintry chandeliers.

Chaos. Chaos. Chaos. The words bloomed in my mind.

I saw him and caught my breath. He was the size of Orion, but he didn't look nearly as tangible. He seemed to be made of smoke, and shadows swept around him. Dark tendrils cloaked him in a wispy toga.

Through the smoky strands, I made out two silver horns gleaming from the top of his head. They curved like a crescent moon, and thorny tattoos curled over his bronze skin. I looked closer. White flowers were threaded in his hair.

"Dying God," said Orion.

"You come into my forest once more." Shadows slid over him, and his voice rang inside my head.

He turned to look at me, his eyes bottomless darkness. I stared into them and felt madness, terror. Uncertainty filled me, and I was no longer sure where I stood. Was there earth beneath my feet? Was this a dream or a nightmare?

"Do you know who you really are yet?" His voice seemed to come from behind me this time, though his lips never moved.

"I'm my mom's daughter." The words came out of my mouth on their own, and I heard them from a distance. My breath puffed around me. "I don't need to know anything else."

Glittering shadows swirled around him. He glided closer now, the movements too smooth to be natural. I stared at his sharp, high cheekbones as he solidified before us, no longer transparent. A dark serpent slid from the darkness behind him and curled around his arm.

He reminded me a little of Orion—terrifying, beautiful.

This solved one mystery. I knew now why these

Puritan women risked their necks to sneak into the woods.

Orion stepped forward, looking a lot more relaxed than I felt. "Will you sever a blood oath I made?" he asked.

"In the old days, people knew how to ask a question of the gods." Tammuz's voice boomed across the forest, a deep growl that shook snowflakes from the boughs. "When people made requests of the gods, they sacrificed something valuable. A lamb, a goat, a cow. A first-born child, delivered into the fiery jaws of Moloch."

A sliver of dread ran through my veins. His dark eyes made me feel unmoored.

Orion raised an eyebrow. "You want me to sacrifice a goat?"

The Dying God seemed to grow larger before us. "No. A goat has no value to you." He looked between the two of us. "I need what you hold most dear. Secrets." He held his arms out to either side. "Confessions. That is what you can give to me."

I hugged myself, shivering. "Confess what?"

Tammuz's eyes locked on me, and he took a step closer, moving with a catlike grace that reminded me of Orion. Behind him, bone-white mushrooms sprouted from the snow where he'd trod.

"You need to admit what you've been running from," his voice boomed. "Confess. Tell me what happened the night your mother died."

I shrank from him like I'd been burned. "I can't confess that because I don't remember."

"Perhaps you didn't see everything." His gaze had turned predatory. "Let me show you what *really* happened."

No. I didn't want to remember. I wanted to turn and run into the shadows instead of facing that night.

Tammuz reached out and touched my collarbone. As his finger grazed my skin, coldness spilled through me.

Out of the corner of my eye, I saw Orion step forward and felt the heat rippling off him. "Don't touch her. What are you doing?"

The god's eyes sparkled. "Taking what's mine."

I glimpsed Orion moving for him, but a vault of star-flecked night swept over me, and they disappeared.

CHAPTER 20—ROWAN

*L*ightning cracked the sky, and for a moment, I glimpsed another figure standing behind him—a horned man with a five-pointed star. My heart skipped a beat.

Lucifer?

But he vanished into the shadows with Orion and Tammuz, leaving me alone in the forest.

Snow swirled around me in wild vortices, then melted. Icicles turned to water, and the earthy smell of spring filled the air. The elms around me turned into pines.

I stared at the landscape, recognition dawning. The gentle roll of the hill and the rocky overhang to my right —this was where it had happened. The same exact place, in a different time.

I felt split in two. Half of me wanted to run from the buried memories of that night, while the other half needed to know what had happened. I needed to know who had killed my mother.

Time slowed. The wind caught in the pines, and the boughs strained. Raindrops slid slowly from the sky.

Fear stole my breath as a figure moved through the shadows. She moved closer, and I saw myself. I was running, red hair frizzy and sweat gleaming on my cheeks.

But where was Mom, and why weren't we together?

I watched myself running, moving in slow motion now. My arms pumped through the air. I ran alone with the precise form of a varsity athlete.

Storm clouds darkened the night sky, and lightning cracked the shadows. A loud clap of thunder rumbled over the forest. Rain hammered me as I ran, and rivulets streamed over the earthy forest floor.

Had I realized how far ahead of Mom I was? Had I even known what I was running from?

Mom couldn't keep up with me. She was a demon without her powers, and I was a trained athlete.

I wanted to close my eyes, but I couldn't. Tammuz wanted me to see this.

What if, when something so devastating happened, it left an imprint on the world? What if horror lingered forever—like Pompeii's victims, eternally contorted in their final moments, tormented tragedies perpetually encased in stone?

At last, Mom ran from the shadows. She looked younger than I remembered, her skin gleaming. Rain drenched her dark hair.

She wore a large backpack, too, and it looked heavy on her shoulders. I remembered now—she'd always kept it by the door, filled with food, water, and a knife. She had a gun at home as well, locked in a safe, for all the good it did when someone came for us. I remembered it all now—there hadn't been time to get the gun.

The forest thinned around me, and a new scene emerged—one with warm light and a familiar blue sofa. My heart ached. We were back now in our house, the bottom-floor rental in Witchcraft Point. With the sound of rain gently pattering the windows, a cozy scene emerged. Fairy lights were strung above the windows. I saw myself on the sofa, surrounded by books, trying to cram for a math test. I sat cross-legged and relaxed. One of Mom's crocheted afghans in light blue lay draped on the sofa behind me, just as it always had been. From the next room, the radio was playing Mozart on a low volume.

This teenage version of me had no idea of what was coming next.

I glanced at the clock on the wall—ten-sixteen at night. The second hand ticked loudly in the room, each strike seeming louder.

This had been my last minute of peace before the world changed completely.

Mom came into the room with a bowl of popcorn. Lightning lit up the sky outside, and she froze, staring out the window, her blue eyes wide. I'd seen those eyes recently—

She dropped the bowl of popcorn. "Run," she

screamed. "Get out! Get your shoes on and run for the car."

I leapt up, trying to see what she'd seen, but nothing was out there except the dark, crooked street in front of our house. Back then, Mom always seemed to be freaking out over nothing, convinced that people were out to get us. In my high school psychology class, I'd learned about paranoid schizophrenia, and I'd wondered if that was what she had. The self-defense classes, the bug out bag, the constant fears that people were watching or following us. And here she was again, screaming that something evil was coming for us. I thought she was imagining it.

I'd argued with her, saying that I wasn't going to leave the house because she *thought* she saw something outside, not when I had more important things to do. I wasn't going to let her paranoia ruin high school for me. As I looked back on myself now, I wanted to scream, *Listen to her, you fucking idiot!*

A math test? *That's* what I'd been worried about?

I felt sick as I watched the argument unfold. Finally, I'd gotten my shoes on, a furious look on my face. We'd left the house through the basement, running into the rainy night. But the argument had flustered her, and she'd forgotten her car keys.

"He's coming!" she'd screamed. "Run into the woods. I'll be right behind you."

My younger self had stared into the shadows, peering from behind a tree. My face paled, jaw dropping open when I glimpsed someone who scared me. I ran, then, sprinting down trails I knew like the back of my hand—every turn, every crook of the path memorized.

Mom started behind me, but she didn't know the way, and she wasn't in shape. She bumped into trees in the dark, her arms grasping at shadows. She couldn't keep up with me, and I'd cost her precious time arguing. On top of that, she'd forgotten the keys, and that was my fault.

And there I was, my younger self, blithely leaving Mom behind to save my own ass. I'd assumed she was right behind me as I ran, but I hadn't stopped to check. Nor had I considered that fact that she couldn't run a five-minute mile like I could, or that she didn't run trails.

I sprinted into the heart of the forest, and the night swallowed me whole.

The murderer was there now, running fast behind Mom.

Hot rage seared me. His mark glowed—a false king. A twisted king, his pale hair streaming behind him as he ran, eyes pure black.

His mark wasn't a five-pointed star like mine or Orion's. He was never destined to rule, never blessed by Lucifer. And this he had to keep hidden.

King Cambriel—my half brother—raced behind Mom, and his forehead glowed with the mark of a golden eye in a triangle.

Mom veered to the right, off the path. Had that been an accident? She was taking herself off the trail, making it harder to run through the brush and brambles.

I had a horrible feeling that her actions were intentional, that she was trying to lure him away from me. She didn't want him to realize I was there, didn't want him to follow me.

Horror slammed into me as I watched him close the distance between them. Flame erupted from his fingertips, touching Mom's hair, which ignited an instant before her clothing went up in flames.

Her screams tore through the quiet forest as her body blazed like a torch. *Mom.* I wish I'd never seen this. Why had the Dying God made me watch this?

King Cambriel shouted a single word, one that punctured the night like a gunshot: *"Bitch!"*

Bitch. *Bitch.* That's what he'd shouted as my mother had burned. I wanted to rip his fucking throat out.

And someday, I would.

The false king—my twisted half brother—fled the way he'd come, scuttling off like a little rat.

The younger me had heard the screams, had seen the blaze of fire in the woods. Even in the driving rain, Mom had burned in flames too hot to be extinguished. I didn't want to hear her wails of pain.

As I watched, my teenaged self ran back to her, my hair as red as the flames. My demon mark glowed on my forehead, a five-pointed star. I was sobbing, the strangled sound nearly inaudible over her agonized screams. I ran closer. Taking my sweatshirt off, I tried to cover her with it. I wanted to stop the burning, but it was too late. She'd fallen silent. Mom lay on the ground, her limbs contorted, the jacket burning along with her. Only my screams filled the air now, and Cambriel probably never realized the difference—we sounded the same, just as anguished.

I watched my younger self stagger away from her body and run. Splashing through a puddle of muddy water, I'd glanced down and seen the demon mark glowing on my forehead. That's when my mind had broken, I think, and I'd lost my memory. It had been too much, the onslaught of horror and dark magic that I didn't understand.

Covered in ash, my younger self had stumbled through the woods like someone already dead, a zombie going through the motions of life.

All that had remained of the memories of that night was the golden star—not who it belonged to or where I'd seen it, but the image of the star. Deep down inside, I'd known that the person with the golden star was responsible for killing Mom. And it was true, wasn't it? My unconscious had put it all together. Somewhere in the hollows of my mind, I realized I was to blame. I'd argued with her. I'd made her forget her keys, and then I'd run away without her. She'd sacrificed herself.

And all along, I'd known I was to blame.

If I hadn't been there, she'd still be alive.

But Cambriel was more guilty than I, and nothing would stop me from seeking the revenge I craved.

I didn't care what Orion wanted. King Cambriel's death would be at my hands.

* * *

THE VISION DISAPPEARED, and I found myself in the underworld once more, now on all fours. The icy forest floor stung my hands.

My entire body was shaking. Nausea overwhelmed me, and I retched. The buttons had popped open on Orion's coat, and the frigid winter air rushed in, chilling my chest. I didn't care. I was too overwhelmed by the horror of what I'd just seen.

Mom. She'd always been the one I'd called for when I was scared.

Someone placed a hand on my back, a gesture that was almost protective. Orion.

Lifting my head, I found the demon god staring down at me like I was an alien species. Some of the nausea passed, and I rocked back onto my heels. Grasping me by the waist, Orion helped me to my feet.

I pulled the edges of the coat together. My mouth still felt watery and sick, and I swallowed hard. I desperately wanted to be out of this place now, curled up in a warm room under a blanket. No—I wanted my mom, but that was stupid because I was an adult, and she was gone.

Shadows writhed and danced around the Dying God, and he smiled at me. "Tell me what you saw."

I took a deep breath. "Here is your confession. The secret you wanted. I remember what happened with my mom. I ruined everything. I argued instead of running when her killer was outside. I didn't believe her, and I made her forget her keys. I ran too fast, and she couldn't keep up. I left her behind." I was speaking in hardly a whisper, but the forest seemed eerily silent. Somehow, my words echoed off the ice. My gaze slid to Orion. "But I wasn't the one who killed her. It was Cambriel. He hated her deeply for some reason. I don't think he had any idea I was there that night."

"Cambriel," Orion repeated, eyes dark. "He wanted to destroy the last Lilu. I'm surprised he let you live, but maybe he thought you could form an alliance."

I wasn't going to say the rest out loud. No reason to let Orion know we would be competing to kill the same person.

Orion folded his arms on his chest, seemingly impervious to the cold. "What secret would you like me to confess?"

The Dying God gave him a knowing smile. "Why don't you tell us what you did in the dungeon?"

Orion went as still as the tree trunks, and shadows breathed around him. "Not *that*."

Not *what*?

Tammuz's green eyes sparkled with delight. "It's hardly a sacrifice if you are willing to give it up."

Why was Orion arguing when I'd relived the worst moment of my life?

Orion slid his hands into his pockets. His expression looked bored, but something about the heat coming off him told me he was raging beneath the surface. "I have plenty of secrets for you to choose from. That one is off limits."

Tammuz shrugged. "You will sacrifice that secret someday. I am in no rush. Time has no meaning here."

Goosebumps rose on my skin, and I had the disturbing feeling we were being watched.

I looked at the woods behind us. Nothing but darkness.

"Relinquish another secret, then." Tammuz's tattoos shifted and slithered over his skin. "I know. Tell me what you plan to do when you are king."

"I plan to get revenge."

"Everyone knows that." Tammuz's voice boomed, and I could tell he was losing patience. "What *exactly* will you do?"

The silence between us felt sharp and spiked.

"I plan to break the curse," said Orion. "The one that strips us of power when we leave the City of Thorns. I plan to free the demons from their gilded prison. We will roam among the mortals as we like."

"And then?" asked the Dying God.

For a heartbeat, Orion met my gaze, then he turned back to Tammuz again, his eyes darkening. Distant shouts rang through the forest, and Orion whirled around, his fingers twitching. The hair rose on the back of my neck, and I turned to look.

Torches flickered in the trees. "Thou foul witch!" someone shouted in the distance. "Come to make the wicked covenant with the devil, to let him poke his cock in your pole hole!"

I grimaced. *Poke his cock in your pole hole?*

"Osborne's best and brightest have arrived," muttered Orion. "This must be Malleus Daemoniorum, here at last."

I glanced down. I was naked except for the enormous coat. I didn't exactly look innocent of the *pole hole* charges. We needed to get out of here before we found ourselves hanged in the underworld.

Glancing up, I saw to my dismay that Tammuz, the Dying God, had disappeared into the dark forest.

The hunters were coming for us, and here in the underworld, we had no weapons or demonic strength to fight back.

*M*y mind swam with visions of Puritan prisons flooded with water and rats, infested with lice and dysentery. On the other hand, their old guns couldn't aim for shit. So that at least was a blessing.

The silvery light of the Dying God must have alerted them, or maybe his impatient shouting at Orion. Now that Tammuz was gone, our best bet was to quietly blend into the forest's shadows.

"Orion," I whispered, "we need to get out of here."

But he didn't look ready to run. He looked like he was waiting for them.

"Orion!" Desperation tightened my gut.

"You should run," he said quietly. "I have plans for Malleus Daemoniorum, and I'm really looking forward to them."

Ah. Were these the hunters who'd come for his family all those centuries ago?

"Yeah, we both should run." I grabbed at his arm, but he was as immobile as stone. "You can't even actually kill them. They're already dead. They'll just come back again. But me? I don't want to die. We could be stuck in this shithole forever."

He quirked an eyebrow, looking irritated. "Has anyone ever told you that you're a buzzkill? Killing Puritans is my idea of a good time. Stop ruining it. They will come back, yes. But I can make them feel terror and indescribable pain. Please don't ruin my good time with all the downsides you keep pointing out." He sighed. "But you should run. It doesn't have anything to do with you, and I don't need your help. We're all on our own here, love. Go on."

I wanted to scream. Instead, I muttered, "Idiot," and took off through the darkness. Maybe he was obsessed with revenge against people who'd died centuries ago, but I wasn't here to get shot and hanged.

I had a strong feeling Orion had forgotten what it was like to fight as a mortal instead of with the godlike strength he possessed in the world of the living.

Gripping my coat tightly, I started running over the frozen ground, snapping twigs.

The winter air bit at my skin, and I had no idea where I was going in the pitch black. Should I head back to town if I could find it?

Sharp regret pierced my chest. What would happen to Orion? What if he couldn't manage the fight on his own? I was leaving someone behind to die again, wasn't I? Just as that thought struck me like an arrow, a scream chilled my blood—an agonized male scream. I felt the air leaving my lungs. *Please, don't let it be Orion.*

I looked back, my heart stuttering at the sight of a body blazing in the distance. I wasn't sure who I was angrier at right now—Orion for refusing to run, or me for leaving him there.

I started sprinting toward him, a bony hand of fear gripping my heart. I had a terrible feeling I'd find him there, half-alive and burning. I could smell it now—the searing flesh, the ashes floating on the wind. *Please,* not Orion…

Despite our twisted relationship and everything he'd said to me, some part of me cared about the dickhead.

Flames bloomed from the forest floor, and as I drew closer, I saw three people illuminated in the light of a burning body. I exhaled when I spied Orion standing with his hands raised, facing me. Blood poured down his forehead.

I lingered in the shadows for a moment, trying to assess the scene.

One of the men had a gun pressed against Orion's head. Another pulled out a rope and pulled Orion's hands behind his back. The third hunter had his back to me.

"Thou wicked, fornicating devil with thy black book!" the man shouted. "Thou shalt be stripped to the waist and whipped through town at the back of a cart."

"Don't threaten me with a good time."

Orion must have used the torch to burn one of them, but he'd been outnumbered. I needed to act now before they bound Orion's hands behind him. For a moment, Orion caught my eyes. He raised an eyebrow nearly imperceptibly.

"We will have thy confession!" shouted the other, trying to bind his arms behind him.

I needed to take down the gunman first.

I looked down and picked up a large rock, jagged and frozen in my fingertips. With the crude weapon in my hands, I darted out of the shadows and brought the rock down hard on the back of the gunman's head. He staggered and whirled, slamming me in the temple with his flintlock. Pain flared through my skull.

But I was still holding my weapon. As panic ignited in my veins, I hit him again with the rock, harder this time.

I heard the crack of bone, and he wavered where he stood, dazed and bleeding. Something caught my eye that made my heart skip a beat. There, on his chest, was the same silver pin that the Corwins wore: a hammer. The hammer of the demons—Malleus Daemoniorum.

The man crumpled to the ground, blood pouring from his head onto the ice. I staggered back, staring at him.

When I looked up again, Orion had freed himself. Wrapping his hands around the throat of one of the mortals, he slammed the man's head into a tree trunk repeatedly, cratering the back of the man's skull.

I gaped at the horror around me: the man engulfed in flames, still twitching, the injured man crawling at my feet, the person Orion was battering to death. The last hunter standing scrambled for the fallen gun. Orion whirled and punched him in the skull with an animal ferocity. He hit him again and again.

Without the magical powers of a demon, killing wasn't quite as clean and tidy as it could be. All this could have been avoided if Orion had run with me, but these messy deaths were his goal.

In a daze, I walked away from the carnage, bile rising in my throat. Vaguely, I wondered if the Dying God would return now and break the oath so that we could get out of here and never come back.

I looked down at myself. Blood streaked my bare skin where my coat had opened, but I wasn't sure if it was mine or the man's I'd just killed.

Since I'd entered the world of demons, I was starting to realize there were only two options in some situations: you could kill or die. And with that in mind, I turned back to the men who lay dying on the forest floor and scanned their bodies for weapons.

The flintlock was large and unwieldy, so I'd leave that behind. The man I'd hit with a rock was still crawling over the ice, although he was half dead. He had another weapon strapped around his waist, a knife, and I pulled it from its sheath. As I did, I felt as if my soul was freezing over.

Goody Putnam had been right. These woods turned people into animals, naked, covered in blood. Stealing weapons from people as they died. Orion was drawing out the death of the man in his hands. I dropped my new weapon into my bag and started walking, not wanting to see any more violence.

A moment later, I heard footfalls behind me and turned to see Orion's silhouette.

His eyes shone brightly in the darkness. "Why did you come back for me?"

My head throbbed, and I wasn't sure I could feel the cold anymore. "I didn't want to leave someone else behind," I said, swallowing hard.

"Wait. Rowan—wait." He stood in front of me, peering down at me. He touched my temple, and his forehead furrowed. "You have a head injury."

"You should see the other guy." My head was pounding, and I wanted to throw up. "He hit me with that flintlock."

"This isn't good. You might be even less fun than you were before." He pulled his hand away. "I can't heal you here."

"Did you forget your lack of magical powers when you decided to take on those armed men?"

He stroked the side of my face again, just below where I'd been struck. Even if he didn't have magic at his fingertips, there was something soothing about his touch. "There is some method to my madness. If they reported back to town and gathered a larger group to hunt us down, we might not leave here alive. We'd be hanged in the town square before we could get back to the turnpike."

"Maybe."

He held my gaze for a moment, then let out a long breath. "I want to get you somewhere warm. Your eyes look unfocused. We'll look for the Dying God again tomorrow." He took my hands between his and chafed them, staring down at my fingertips. "You're starting to get frostbite."

My thoughts were going dim, like someone had covered them in a dark, fuzzy blanket, and I felt myself falter.

Orion scooped me up in his arms, and I wrapped my arms around his neck, warming myself against his body. As he carried me, I rested my head against his chest, listening to his heartbeat. "Why don't you feel the cold?" I mumbled.

"It was always cold in the dungeon," he whispered, picking up his pace.

I half wondered how he was going to explain the state of us, but with his warmth enveloping me, I was staring to drift off. I listened to the sound of Orion's heart, feeling strangely safe wrapped in the arms of my enemy.

CHAPTER 22—ROWAN

T woke naked in Orion's arms.

He gave me a crooked half smile. "There you are."

Frowning, I surveyed the candlelit room around me. Thick wooden beams crossed the ceiling above Orion's head, and the walls were plain white. A four-poster bed stood in the center of the room, and a copper tub steamed beneath a shuttered window. A fire burned in a hearth, filling the room with the scent of burning cedar.

My head was still bleary. "Why am I naked, Orion?"

In here, the ceilings were so short, he had to hunch. "Because I'm going to get the blood off you and thaw you out."

Carefully, he lowered me into the warm bathwater. At first, the shock of the heat on my frozen fingers and toes made my breath catch, and it almost stung. It felt like my fingers were swelling, but within moments, the warmth was pure bliss. I sank deeper into the water and rubbed my fingers together. "Where are we?" I asked.

"The Putnam Tavern."

"Ah, you charmed her again, did you? How did you explain that I was naked and covered in blood?"

"I told her that we and the other Malleus Daemoniorum members found the evil in the forest, and that a terrible fight ensued. But she really wanted to know about your wicked thoughts. She suggested that tomorrow, you should make a public penance for your unnatural desires."

I stared at him. "I believe you had some of your own unnatural desires."

"Always." He leaned down next to the tub, a cloth in his hand. Gently, he washed my face, dabbing the cloth into the water.

But that was all it was, wasn't it? We'd jumped all over each other because we were Lilu, out of control in the magic of the woods. I sank deeper into the water. "Are you going to fill me in about your revenge plan? Why was Tammuz asking about that?"

I stared at his achingly beautiful face, at the silvery hair that skimmed his sharp cheekbones. His eyebrows were thick and dark, a sharp contrast to the paleness of his haunted eyes. "I don't like to discuss nightmares directly before bed."

He washed the blood from my skin, then pulled the cloth away, his gaze shuttered. "I'm going to see if Goody Putnam has some clothes you can borrow."

When he left the room, the ache in my chest

increased. No matter what happened between us, he would never completely trust me. And he'd never apologized for the things he'd said.

When the bathwater started to cool, I rose. I didn't see a towel—in fact, I wasn't sure they had them in the old days. Crossing to the roaring fire, I dried my naked body by the flames. I won't lie, I loved the heat of the fire, but it was hard not to think of this inn as a *slight* death trap without fire magic to protect me. This place was lit by hearths and candles and had zero fire alarms. When my body had dried off, I put my underwear back on, the only item of clothing I still had.

Normally, before I went to sleep, I'd scan through my phone looking at Instagram or text messages, or something with a connection to the outside world. Something to make me feel less lonely. But I didn't have that here, so I grabbed my father's note out of my backpack and slid under the sheets.

I unfolded it, staring at my father's neat, blocky handwriting.

Long live King Nergal. Long live King Nergal. Long live King Nergal.

I traced my fingertips over his words. It wasn't exactly easing my loneliness, but it was sparking my curiosity.

Why the hell would someone write this and save it?

As I touched the letter, I felt something in the paper— the tiniest of ridges. I frowned and held the note up to the firelight. My breath caught. There, tiny pinpricks of orange light streamed through the paper—little holes that formed delicate letters.

My heart sped up. This was a primitive system for encoding a message.

Pulse racing, I deciphered the contents of a letter addressed to my mom.

Aria,

I fear my time here is running out. The false prince, my disloyal son, is impervious to my threats to allow us to return. He does not know of our beloved creation, Rowan. I have spoken with the Dying God. He confirmed our fears. If the Lord of Chaos succeeds, the mortal realm will burn. Only Mortana's ka can reign. Only the third Lightbringer can restore us. I will return to you as soon as I can.

—Moloch

I read the letter again and again, trying to make sense of the words. I was shocked to see the Lord of Chaos mentioned, and the Dying God too, And my name! For the first time, my suspicions had been confirmed—Aria and Moloch were my true parents.

My thoughts spun, and I glanced at the door. How much time did I have until Orion returned?

Some of this was simple. The false prince, his disloyal son. That was King Cambriel, my half brother.

My heart was slamming against my ribs.

Three golden Lightbringer stars—the marks of Lucifer. Me, Orion, and—Mortana? They'd referred to us like we were two different people.

If the Lord of Chaos succeeds, the mortal realm will burn.

That…did not sound great.

Here it was at last, some proof that I was not who Orion thought I was. My heart stuttered to life as I read the words again.

Only Mortana's ka can reign...

I was the third Lightbringer.

But I had no idea what a ka was. An identical daughter? And why did he call me a "beloved creation"? That wasn't really a normal way to refer to a family member. It sounded like Frankenstein's monster.

I closed my eyes, and the vision of Cambriel played in my mind again. According to this letter, my parents had been threatening him. And if I had to guess, they had the same leverage as Orion. They were threatening to let the world know he wasn't the true king. And unlike Orion, they were easier to kill to get rid of the evidence.

Footfalls creaked outside, and I folded the note up again, shoving it into my little leather bag. The door opened, and Orion crossed into the room, a dress slung over his arm—and a shawl this time. *Nice.*

I watched him, an idea blooming in my mind. I had to take the crown from him. There were only two people I'd ever truly trusted in this world: my mom and Shai. Mom believed I should be queen. And you know what? I'd make a better ruler than he would. He was completely unhinged.

I watched Orion as he pulled off his shirt, and the firelight wavered over his powerful body.

I wanted to tell him—at last, I had proof that I wasn't Mortana. My parents thought we were two different people, like I'd been trying to tell him all along. Every childhood memory I treasured was real, not a fabrication. The Christmas mornings with just me and Mom—all of that was real.

But given what else this letter included, I knew I had to keep it a secret. No reason to let him know I was coming for his throne.

I pulled the blankets over my shoulders and rolled over, staring into the flames. Flickering in the dancing tongues of fire, I thought I saw forms moving. Writhing.

Orion and my parents had been blackmailing the king in their own ways—Orion for money, my parents for their own goals. But unlike Orion, they hadn't been strong enough to fight him off.

Just like my mom had sacrificed herself in the woods, I wondered if my father had died to save me. Maybe they wanted *me* back in the City of Thorns with them. As demons, we were safest there.

With the blankets tucked around me, I closed my eyes. Images were burned into my mind—Cambriel, with his glowing sigil, had ripped out my father's heart in front of his house, then burned his body to hide the evidence. Cambriel wasn't going to allow them to blackmail him.

If the Lord of Chaos succeeds, the mortal realm will burn.

Maybe, now that I was a demon, I hungered for power, too. Not because I wanted to burn the world down, like Orion. It seemed the only way to stay safe. When you had no power at all, the world chewed you up and spit you out.

I felt the mattress sag as Orion got in and his body

warmed the bed. I stole a quick look at him. Firelight danced back and forth over his enormous muscles.

"I don't suppose Goody Putnam had pajamas for me?" I asked.

He slowly turned his sultry gaze on me, and I felt my core grow tight. "I'm afraid not, love. In any case, Goody Putnam argued that you won't need clothes for your public penance tomorrow. I'm quite looking forward to it. It will be a delightful event for Osborne."

"She's really into this." I stared at him. "She's the kinkiest person in this place."

A knowing smile. "Not sure about that. I was locked in a dungeon most of my life. I've hardly had the chance to explore yet."

He was flirting with me, but I wasn't going to give him the chance to hurt me again.

I narrowed my eyes at him. "As I recall, you said you felt nothing for me and that your attraction to me was the desperation of a Lilu to feed, nothing more. I thought we both understood that's all this was. That what happened in the forest was *just* the effect of magic. We don't like one another, right?"

He looked at me, and for a moment, I thought I saw a flash of hurt in his eyes. Then a bland smile appeared on his face, his eyes half-lidded with indifference. "Right. Like I said before, we are all alone in this world."

That was a very Orion outlook.

Using the blankets, I formed a barrier between us. He looked on with amusement as I tucked a pillow between our bodies.

"Have you ever heard of something called a ka?" I asked carefully.

A line formed between his eyebrows. "Like an automobile?"

Damn. "No, not a car—ka. I thought it was a demon thing."

"Never heard of it. Why are you asking?"

"It was something I saw in the vision," I lied. "The vision said I was Mortana's ka. It said there are three of us with the star of Lucifer."

He stared at me like he was trying to read me, his eyes strangely sorrowful in the firelight. Shadows danced over his high cheekbones. "An interesting theory, but one of two things are true. Either this is real and you are not Mortana—"

"Yeah. That."

"—or you could be Mortana, and this is another one of your many, *many* seductive lies." He reached for my face and brushed his thumb over my lower lip—a slow, sensual stroke. "I'm inclined to think the latter, love."

Inside, I felt something snap, like a twig cracking in a fire. "That was my last attempt to convince you."

He leaned in even closer and whispered next to my ear. "Good. It's the hope that kills you, isn't it?"

I pushed him away from me. "Stay on your side of the barrier. Now, if we both have the mark of Lucifer, aren't you worried I might beat you to the throne?"

He quirked a smile. "I'm not worried about you," he purred. "You don't have it in you. Not anymore."

Well, that sounded like a fucking challenge, didn't it?

I slid further under the covers, rolling away from him on my side of the barrier.

Orion made me thankful for one thing. His patronizing attitude was going to make it that much easier to ruin his dreams and take what he thought belonged to him.

And make it mine.

CHAPTER 23—ROWAN

I woke with a strange tingling in my body and an icy chill in the room. With chattering teeth, I rubbed my arms, trying to get warmer. The fire must have gone out, and frost had settled over the chamber, encasing the bed.

But it wasn't just the cold, was it? Powerful magic wrapped around me, vibrating on my skin under the blankets. There it was again—that feeling that someone was watching me.

I hugged myself and slowly opened my eyes. A feeling of dread slid through me, and I sat up straight, the breath leaving my lungs.

The Dying God sat in a chair in the corner of the room, darkness curling around him. From the fireplace, the embers cast a warm glow that tinged the smoke with red. The Dying God's dark eyes were locked on me, gleaming and forest green.

Not creepy at all.

"What the *fuck*?" I blurted, holding the blankets over my chest.

Orion shot upright in the bed next to me, then saw the Dying God and relaxed. "Ah. Tammuz." He yawned. "If you are hoping for a threesome, I'm afraid it won't happen." He nodded at me. "She's a bit annoyed with me."

"I'm here for your confession," said Tammuz. "And then I will destroy your blood oath. Tell me, now, what do you plan to do as king?" The sound of his deep, growling voice boomed off the walls. Surely Goody Putnam would wake? Not that she'd be disappointed to find him here.

Orion went very still. "Revenge."

From the darkness, the Dying God appeared again, closer this time, at the foot of the bed. "More."

Orion sighed. "I've already killed King Nergal, and I plan to kill the other demons who participated long ago. I will find them all. I will reclaim everything they stole."

The Dying God faded into darkness again, but his voice whispered next to my head. "More."

I practically jumped out of the bed.

How did he know that it didn't end there? I was starting to get the impression he already knew the answers to the questions he asked.

"The massacre began with the mortals," said Orion, his voice cold and quiet. "And now they keep us trapped within the city gates. We cannot leave the City of Thorns without losing our power. They have dominion over us. They fear what we are because we are better than they are. We are stronger, smarter, more beautiful. When I am

176

king, I will find the spell that keeps us trapped and break it. Demons will be free to roam the world once more. Lucifer urbem spinarum libarabit. The Lightbringer will set the City of Thorns free. That is me. I will liberate my kind. And I will make sure that no one capitulates to the mortals again, sacrificing our own."

A cold shiver ran down my spine at his words. I'd seen them carved in the dungeon the first night we'd met. Liberation should be joyful—so why did he make it sound so terrifying?

"The mortals were the reason King Nergal slaughtered us," Orion's voice was glacial. "King Nergal, who sired me—"

"Did he?" For the first time, Tammuz sounded angry, and his guttural rage sent electric fear through my veins. I still couldn't see him, which only made him more terrifying. A growl trembled over the room, making the bed shake, and the sound of creaking wood grew louder.

"Yes. It is why I was marked as the true heir. It's why I could kill him. But he was a slave to the mortals. A coward. And one day, I will open the gates to Hell. I will unleash my demon brothers and sisters on the world of the mortals, and we will live like we did in the old days. Once, the mortals worshipped us. Now, they celebrate our demise. I will make them feel true terror. I will sever their heads and stick them on pikes. I will make them feel what I felt, such horror that they're not even sure if the world around them is real. I will burn the world for seven days, and demons will rise from the ashes anew."

Nausea rose in my gut. "Holy shit, Orion. The people

177

responsible died centuries ago. They're not the same as the Puritans you hate. You can't just cut random people's heads off."

He shrugged, looking completely unperturbed by this particular detail. "I will begin with the demon hunters, then. They are the same."

"You'll start with the demon hunters," I replied. "But where will you end?"

A line formed between his eyebrows. "Wherever I want it to end. When I am satiated."

With his charm and his easy grace, I'd never realized how fucked up he was. Bloodlust ran through his veins, and he would never be appeased. I couldn't say he hadn't warned me. He'd told me since day one that he was terrible.

Of *course* he was a head case. No one could spend their entire life in a dungeon and turn out normal.

I stared at him. "So you would murder thousands of people who had nothing to do with what you're angry about."

His eyes grew shadowed. "Yes. You're not going to tell me that mortals are better than they once were, are you? Do you think they've suddenly become *nice*? The past hundred years of history tells me otherwise." He turned back to the end of the bed, where Tammuz had been. "Will you break the blood oath now? You had my confession."

I couldn't help but wonder why Tammuz demanded this confession if he already knew the truth. In fact, the note said that he'd told my parents exactly this—if the Lord of Chaos reigns, the mortal realm will burn.

There was only one reason for these confessions, then. Tammuz wanted me to hear it. He wanted me to stop Orion.

The Dying God crossed over to Orion and touched the center of his forehead. Silver light slid over Orion's body like water, streaming from the top of his head down his powerful shoulders, biceps, and back. Orion closed his eyes, his muscles tensing.

I looked down and saw the same thing—silver light sliding over me. An overwhelming sense of calm washed over me. The Dying God's magic was like the caress of a gentle wind, and I was caught in the crossfire, imbued with the same magic.

In the hollows of my mind, I heard him speak to me. "You are free of your blood oath, Rowan," he said.

Tammuz disappeared, leaving us alone again. Holy shit. Why had he broken *my* oath as well? A sense of freedom and calm washed over me, and I couldn't keep my eyes open any longer.

I sank into the mattress, the soft pillow. The bed felt glorious to my tired muscles, and my body melted into it.

* * *

WHEN I WOKE AGAIN, the barrier between us had disappeared, and Orion was curled around me, his length pressed against my backside. He held me close to him protectively.

Don't get too used to this, Rowan. It's not real, even if it feels real.

I nudged him with my elbow, moving him away. "Orion. The barrier."

I turned to look at him, and he propped his head on his hand, staring at me with sleepy eyes. "We did it." His smile was satisfied. "We broke the oath."

A shard of rosy light pierced the gloom, and I turned to see the sun rising outside. Dawn was breaking already.

"Now," said Orion, "it's time for you to fulfill your promise. Don't think I forgot."

I glanced at the shadowy space where the Dying God had been standing. I'd heard him tell me that he'd broken mine, too. Now it was time to test it out.

I met Orion's gaze. "There's a book in his room," I lied. "During the day, one of his guards carries it around, but they're always switching guards, so it's hard to know which one might have it. But at night, Cambriel sleeps with it under his pillow. Get it from him when he's fast asleep. Destroy the book, and you can kill him that way."

"And your parents wrote all this down?"

"They wanted someone to kill him." I shrugged. "I guess it'll be you."

CHAPTER 24—ROWAN

*C*lad in Goody Putnam's scratchy wool dress, I crossed the icy fields with Orion, striding past the hanging women once more. The milky morning light shone brightly on the frosted grass and sparkled on ice-encased trees.

In the distance, the row of wooden pikes protruded from the frozen gray earth like rotten teeth. And beyond those pikes, the caves of Purgatory loomed. Orion nodded. "As soon as we cross this turnpike, we are back. We don't have to go through Purgatory this time."

I let Orion take the lead as we got closer to the pikes. Sliding the backpack off my shoulders, I reached inside for the knife.

Just at the turnpike itself—the barrier to the veil, Orion turned to look at me, one foot over the edge.

I pressed the tip of the knife against his heart and stared up into his eyes. "I'm sorry, Lord of Chaos. But this is where we part."

He glanced down at the knife. When he looked back at me, a faint smile dimpled his cheek. "Well, this is certainly unexpected."

"Take one step back, Orion. Like I said, I need more time here."

The wind ruffled his silver hair, and his eyes pierced me. "Why?"

I smiled back. "Just some things I need to take care of. I'd ask you to help, but I really don't think you have it in you. Now why don't you take a step back and leave the important stuff to me? I am, after all, the Lightbringer."

He arched a quizzical eyebrow. "Is this what it feels like to be patronized?"

"It's actually very enjoyable, you know. I can see why you do it. Now fuck off, love." I pressed the knife a little harder against him. It was, according to my guess, just above his heart. I didn't want to kill him, of course. I wanted him trapped on the other side of Purgatory. "Please don't make me end your life."

He sighed and leaned down, his face close to mine. "Well, I guess it's a good thing you're not capable of it, then. But why, exactly, would you want to stay *here* without me? You really don't think you can—"

He reached for my wrist, but I headbutted him—hard, slamming my forehead into his nose. He stumbled back and disappeared in a flash of light.

I stared at the space where he'd been and rubbed the ache in my forehead.

"Thanks, Mom," I whispered, "for making me take those self-defense classes."

* * *

IN GOODY PUTNAM'S INN, I sipped a pewter flagon of hot beer. I'd been here all day. On the one hand, she kept asking me to make a public penance. On the other, it was nice and warm inside, with a cozy fire, hot beer, and soup.

Sharp-eyed, Goody Putnam approached me with an expression of concern. She leaned over the table, eyes darting in either direction. "Goodman Ashur told me what happened to the hunters last night. But why would a woman be among them? It isn't natural."

Without Orion here to charm her, she made me pay double for food and drink. Good thing I was the one carrying the coins.

I put my finger to my lips. She knew I'd taken a vow of silence, and it saved me from having to fake an accent —and also from trying to figure out the old-fashioned grammar. From what I could tell, they said "you" when they were being polite and "thou" when they wanted to scream that you were a devil-shagging whore. But I didn't quite have the intricacies down, so it was better to keep my mouth shut.

She narrowed her eyes and pressed her palms on the table as she leaned closer. "Were you with the Malleus Daemoniorum, Goody Ashur, or did you separate your-selves from them for your own safety? Maybe you saw the devil?"

There it was again—that strange name. I simply put my finger to my lips again piously.

She nodded slowly. "Aye, the devil murdered our demon-finders. Burned them. Hacked them. Feasted on their bones. True evil." She bowed her head. "You are blessed to have survived."

Not exactly, Goody Putnam.

* * *

THE FLAGON WARMED my hands as I entered the dark woods. I'd spent all day at the inn, filling my stomach and warming myself by the fire.

As I'd walked through the forest, the setting sun had tinted the clouds with shades of periwinkle and cherry. With night falling, I wound my way between elms and yews, searching for the Dying God again.

Once the daylight disappeared completely, silver light streamed through the tree branches, casting glittering flecks of silver on the mossy earth.

The deeper I walked, the colder I felt, and my breath clouded around me. But the shawl was a huge improvement, warm wool that covered my back and shoulders.

The forest grew darker as I searched, and a chorus of whispers echoed off the trees—my own name repeated over and over until it started to sound meaningless and bizarre.

At last, I sensed the charged magic of the Dying God. A low, guttural growl trembled through the boughs, making my hair stand on end.

The symbols of Tammuz carved through the darkness, bright slashes of light from the shadows. Dread turned my blood to ice, and my heart started to race.

"Tammuz…" I whispered his name, waiting for him to appear. Then, a little louder, "Tammuz."

Cold wind rushed between the trees, stinging my cheeks and fingers, and darkness streamed around me, blocking out the moonlight. A rush of primordial power skittered up my spine, making my back arch, and I nearly dropped the shawl.

It took me a moment to recall the words of the strange spell Orion had uttered last night. Even if I didn't know what the words meant, they'd been branded in my mind.

I spoke the words, power surging through my veins and lighting me up like the symbols around me.

From the dark earth, a ring of ivory mushrooms sprouted, and from a glittering swirl of snow, the Dying God slowly appeared in the center of the ring. Smoky shadows twined with the snowflakes.

"You summon me again, Lightbringer." His deep, growling voice trembled over the forest.

My breath shallowed. "Did you want me to hear what Orion will do if he becomes king?"

Tammuz faded into the darkness, reappearing behind my shoulder. "Yes," he whispered in my ear.

I jumped at the unexpected closeness and turned to look at him. His eyes were deep wells of darkness and pain.

My heart slammed against my ribs.

He flickered away into darkness, but his voice

rumbled out of the shadows. "You must fight for the crown."

My fingers tightened on my flagon. Right now, I felt unsteady on my feet, unsure if this was all a strange dream. "Can you tell me what I am? And why there's more than one Lightbringer?"

"You are Mortana's ka." His voice came from inside my own mind.

"What is a ka?"

A dark, throbbing sound pounded from the ground beneath my feet. "An essence. A spirit. A ka lives in a person's body, then separates at death. The ka is a double, and it travels to the double world." He was standing behind me again, coldness radiating over me. "A ka lives on forever. You were here, once. Mortana's double in the world of death."

Fear slid around me, ice-cold. My teeth chattered uncontrollably. "Orion said he didn't think demons had souls."

"That's because he feels like he died a long time ago."

"So I'm Mortana?"

"No. Mortana once knew a spell for forgetting. She came here to these woods to conduct it." His voice echoed off the rocks and trees. "She removed her ren— her true name. It's the part of the soul that contained her memories. But in the process, she removed her ka, her life spirit, and her akh, her intelligence. She became an empty vessel, wandering through the forest mindlessly until the mortals captured her and killed her. After they hanged her, they soon forgot she existed at all."

That was what I'd seen in the vision, then. Mortana's death—here. "And where do I come from?"

"Her ka remained—her double. With my help, your parents brought you into the world of the living as a new person, with a new akh and ren. As Mortana's double, you are destined to rule as well."

I sucked in a deep breath. "If I have her essential spirit, wouldn't I be evil, too?"

He appeared before me, the shadows lapping at the air around him. "No one is born evil. Your mother raised you with love. Mortana was raised in the court of the mad King Azriel, separated from your parents. She grew up in a poisoned garden, twisted and sadistic."

I felt the air leave my lungs as I tried to wrap my head around it.

The world seemed to tilt beneath my feet. "Why? Why are you doing all of this?"

"Chaos." The words echoed around the grove, and I heard the flutter of wings and rustling leaves as birds took flight from the trees. "Lucifer, my twin, marked one to rule—Mortana. But Lucifer is a god of order and light. I am the god of chaos and shadows, the Night Bringer." He shimmered in and out of view. "The universe was made from chaos, and to chaos it will return. Order is as ephemeral as ashes scattered on the wind. It is not the natural state."

I breathed in deeply. "So you wanted a competition for the throne to make things interesting? And you want me to have a fighting chance against Orion."

"Yes." He was standing before me once more, shining

in the dark grove. His body was enormous, towering over me. His coppery skin looked as solid as marble.

"Orion is the Lord of Chaos." I thought of Tammuz's reaction when Orion mentioned his father. "Orion's mother knew you. Any chance Orion is your son?"

"Yes," he hissed, "and the name he gave you is not his real one. He hardly remembers who he is."

My breath caught. "Why is he so convinced he was Nergal's son?"

"Because of the star he bears, marking him as heir to the throne. But Nergal had no children, no natural heir. Orion is a Lightbringer because I chose him as one." Runes of light slashed the air around him. "Rowan," he boomed, "ask what you came here to ask."

My throat tightened. "If you want me to have a fighting chance at the throne, I need your help. Orion is right—I can't fight like he can. I don't connect to my demon side, and I still feel like a mortal. Can you help me?"

A subtle smile played about his lips. "Welcome home, ka."

ammuz turned and started walking away from me into the dark. "You fear death. That is your weakness."

I stared at him. "Everyone is afraid of death. It's a basic part of human evolu—" I stopped myself. "Right. I'm not human. Surely demons fear death, too. It seems like an important part of staying alive."

He turned to face me again. "The Lord of Chaos does not. If anything, he envies the dead. But you are soft, Rowan. You are weak. You will fail."

Rude. My throat tightened. "Okay. I need to be less afraid of death." I closed my eyes. "But there's the fear of pain—"

"Why fear something that is over so quickly?"

"And then there's the fear of what comes after. Do I end up here? Do I just stop existing?"

"Why fear nonexistence?" he asked. "Do you feel afraid when you think of the past, before you existed?"

"No."

"Your body will feed the earth, as mine does once a year. Mushrooms grow from my flesh, and their mycelium spread beneath the forest floor, wrapping around the roots of trees that drink the light of the sun. Death gives birth to life, Rowan, darkness to light, and the spirit lives on in the cycle of life and death."

I heard distant shouts in the woods.

I knew things repeated here, that the dead came back to life. But were the Malleus Daemoniorum already back? I turned, catching sight of torches that pierced the dark.

The shouts were growing louder now, and I recognized Goody Putnam's voice. I froze, my heart rate speeding up as I stared between the tree trunks. I couldn't let them catch me here with the Dying God himself. So many torches, like moving fireflies. This wasn't just the Malleus Daemoniorum. This was an angry mob. How many mortals had come into the forest?

I turned back to the Dying God, but he was gone. Darkness had enveloped the woods completely, clouds covering the moon and stars.

Either Tammuz had ditched me again or he knew I couldn't be seen with him. But all of this was deeply inconvenient when I needed his help.

I turned and started hurrying away from the oncoming mob. If they managed to find me, I would explain that this was part of my penance—wandering in the cold woods. I turned to look over my shoulder. Why were they running so fast?

"Witch!" I heard the shout echo through the forest—Goody Putnam again. "She was consorting with the devil when the Malleus Daemoniorum were murdered!"

My chest went tight. What the hell, Goody Putnam?

"Where are you?" I whispered frantically to the Dying God.

At least these people had torches, which meant I should be able to keep away from them in the shadows. I hurried over the knotted tree roots, over the icy rocks. They seemed to be homing in on me with a surprising amount of accuracy, considering it was pitch black here.

"The spirit leads me to her," shouted a man's voice.

What the hell? I reached into my backpack, feeling around for the hilt of the knife. This would be a fantastic time to have my magic.

With a racing heart, I looked around for a place to hide, but I could hardly see in the darkness. Gripping my knife, I sneaked behind a large oak and peered around the trunk, watching the torches growing larger. The shouts were growing closer now, the mob hurling insults at me. "Thou foul witch. Thou demoness. Thou hast returned!"

They were coming at me with the *thou*s again. Rude.

Someone was calling me a whore. I wasn't quite sure how that fit into the scenario, but it seemed to be a classic go-to insult whenever men were angry at women.

My only defense was the darkness, but it wasn't slowing them down a bit. As they started to close in again, I realized I had to move. I took one step. Two steps. My foot snapped a twig. I froze. Gunshots rang out behind me.

What had suddenly sent them after me? Had Goody Putnam suspected me?

"Kill her!" A male voice, full of primal rage. "She murdered the Malleus Daemoniorum!"

Bone-deep fear charged my body, and I tried to run through the trees, but the ground was uneven.

There were too many of them, their shouts growing louder, closer—

Another gunshot, and pain exploded through the back of my left shoulder. I grunted, reaching for it. Agony electrified my body, and I fell to my knees. I had to fight now.

A primal desperation for survival took over, forcing me to my feet. I turned, wildly flailing with my knife as the torches and bodies surrounded me. I stabbed someone, but a blade cut through my side. Another blow on the back of my head, and I lost my footing. They were all around me, these men in dark coats and tall hats.

One more crack to my skull, and my world went silent.

* * *

I WOKE with the early morning sunlight streaming over me, startled to find that I was still alive.

It took a moment for the pain to register. And when it did, I felt as if a knife were splitting my skull open from the back to the front. I tried to raise my hand to my head, but my arms had been tied tightly behind my back. My shoulder muscles burned. I was lying flat on something hard, like a bench.

Above me, red and gold leaves trembled on a tree branch. A gust of wind swept over me, catching the leaves and rolling them in the air. I breathed in deeply, my stomach turning. It smelled like death here.

And then I noticed something moving in the corner of my vision. Dread sank into my lungs. A noose dangled from the branch, swaying forlornly overhead.

I'd been warned. *Do you want to see how you'll die?* Maybe that wasn't Mortana's death I'd seen. *Fuck.*

Above me, the bough groaned in the wind, a haunting sound. I shifted, trying to sit up to get a better view.

"The demon wakes!" The deep male voice sent shockwaves of fear through my nerves.

I scrambled to get up, but with my arms tied, I was unsteady. On my knees now, I took in the horrifying scene around me. I was kneeling in a rickety cart that was rambling up Gallows Hill.

Where hundreds of years later a Dunkin' would stand —and my old powder-blue home—a grim crowd gathered. Men, women, and children glared at me, and Goody Putnam stood in the front row.

She pointed at me. "I saw her! I saw Goody Ashur signing the devil's book!" She continued to point at me, her expression furious. "I saw a goat sucking on her witch's teat!"

Four hundred years ago, the mortals hunted down others of their kind based on hearsay, paranoia, and the ravings of attention-seekers. Right now, an actual demon stood before them, and they were still spouting bullshit because there was no devil's book or teat-sucking goat. This would be hilarious if it weren't so terrifying.

Behind them, in the distance, I could see the road I'd walked in on, and the old Osborne Woods. A black house stood before the forest, and smoke rose from a chimney.

When I turned to look behind me, I saw the four women's corpses rotting at the ends of ropes, their bodies gray and purple. Like me, their hands had been bound behind their backs before they'd died. The stench of death was overpowering.

To my left, two horses were hitched to the cart. A man stood near them, dressed in black with a wide white collar and a dark tapered hat.

I tried to stand again, but the pain shot through my head, so sharp that nausea started to take over. I doubled over, vomiting onto the wooden cart. My hands involuntarily tried to jerk forward as I was sick, but the ropes kept them bound. I nearly lost my balance. When I'd stopped vomiting, I wiped my mouth off on my shoulder.

I straightened again, staring out at the crowd. Goody Putnam took a step forward, pointing at me. "She bewitched the chowder. She made me feel lustful things."

The sharp forms of this particular terror were starting to take shape. I understood what was about to happen, and I could hardly breathe. I *had* been warned. Why hadn't Tammuz stepped in if he'd wanted me to have a chance against Orion?

"I didn't bewitch anything!" I shouted. "Don't I get a trial? A trial!"

"Listen to her strange manner of speech!" someone shouted.

The man in black nodded at two men in the crowd—a ruddy-cheeked man with a dark beard and a broad-shouldered man with piercing eyes. The two of them marched closer to the cart, then climbed inside.

"I haven't bewitched anyone or touched a goat. I swear to you," I said. "A trial! Even the Puritans had trials."

One of the men grabbed me hard, and the other slid the noose around my neck. I struggled against them, but without my arms, there wasn't much I could do. Once they'd secured the noose around my neck, the two men jumped from the cart.

With a hammering heart, I glanced at the horses. Once someone whipped them, the cart would disappear beneath me. My neck would break if I was lucky. I'd strangle to death if I was not. That could take twenty minutes.

At executions in the old days, loved ones would tug on the condemned person's feet to make it go faster if the victim's neck didn't break. What a terrible task that would be. Maybe it was a mercy no one I knew was here, a grim sort of blessing not to have family around to watch you die.

I wasn't really going to die, though, was I? This couldn't happen.

I surveyed the angry crowd in front of me.

"Demon, demon," they were shouting. "Wicked temptress!"

I struggled against my bound wrists, the ropes chafing my skin. I glanced down, my heart hammering, as I spotted the frozen, rocky earth beneath the cart. In the vision, I'd seen my own feet dangling above that very ground.

"Judge Corwin!" Goody Putnam's voice rose above the din. "Make her confess!"

The man in black stepped in front of me, wearing a black coat and a silver hammer pin. He clutched a black book to his chest. His eyes were a cold, flinty gray. The family resemblance was unmistakable. *Corwin.*

He looked every bit as nice as his descendant, Jack Corwin.

My heart skipped a beat. I looked out over the angry crowd as if I were expecting someone to ride up and save me, but I saw only the forest.

Tammuz, you chaotic bastard. Was this all you'd wanted from me? To die here surrounded by fucking morons?

The judge held up a hand, and the crowd went silent. He grinned, exposing long, yellowed teeth. "Confess, thou witch, and we might free thee."

That was a trick, wasn't it? If I told them I was a demon, they wouldn't let me go. They'd kill me. "I'm not a demon," I said desperately. That was a lie, of course. "I don't have any magical power." That part was true, at least at the moment.

"Didst thou kill four men last night?" the judge bellowed, steam rising from his lips.

"No!" I shouted.

True. I'd only killed one of them.

His eyes narrowed. "And didst thou kill thine own kin? Because thou wert afraid?"

The temperature plummeted, and I started to shake. The cart was rattling beneath me, and the sky started to darken. Charcoal gray clouds were rolling in strangely fast. Thunder rumbled overhead.

I stared at him, too stunned to speak. How did he know that? Did he know I'd left Mom behind in these woods?

"Didst thou kill thine own kin?" asked the judge. "Thou hast chosen thine own life! Thy soul art corrupted with evil. Woe be unto thee with wickedness in thy blood!"

How the fuck would he know that? I thought the underworld had been frozen in time. He was talking about things from a few years ago.

"Confess!" he roared. "And we will set thee free. We ask only that thou tellest the truth. Tell us all the wicked ways thou hast saved thyself, demon. How thou hast sacrificed thy kin."

What the *hell*?

The crowd started jeering again.

I shouted at them, "I should get a trial. Everyone had trials. We are English subjects. It's in the Magna Carta, for fuck's sake!" My voice echoed. My panic had me swearing at a group of bloodthirsty Puritans.

The judge's hammer pin gleamed in the winter sun. His grin widened, lupine. "Thou hath pleasure in thy wickedness."

"The keys," I said quietly. "Do you want to hear about the keys?"

The judge's smile faded completely. "Speak not in thy demon tongue! Thou shalt not suffer a demon to live!"

He lifted the whip and cracked it against the horses. They started to run, taking the cart with them and ripping it out from underneath me.

If you were lucky, your neck snapped, but mine didn't. The rough rope crushed my throat, and my legs kicked helplessly in the air. All the blood rushed into my head, and my body commanded me to live, even though I was dying.

My lungs were going to explode.

Never in my life had I understood how precious it was to breathe, how glorious it was to take oxygen deep inside your chest. Never had I felt so desperate to live, to savor every moment. Maybe they would still let me out of this. Maybe they were trying to scare me before the trial.

I wanted to dial back the clock, to relish each second from my past.

Ten-sixteen at night. I wanted to go back before that moment.

Memories exploded in my mind, and I felt myself tugged into the past—lying in the grass in summer and watching the clouds sliding overhead, my fingers sticky with melted popsicles. One day, I'd tried on my mom's bra and stuffed it with socks. The boy next door told me the big kids called them *tits*.

The summer sky melted away, and I was jumping into the town pool, making as big a splash as possible. The lifeguard blew the whistle. I'd nearly hit someone.

"Murderess!" The word ripped the memories from my mind again.

I'd been so sure the Dying God had wanted me for something, that he'd had a plan. I'd been *certain*.

Another memory: graduation from elementary school, when Mom took me to my favorite burger place and let me order whatever I wanted, and I had a chocolate milkshake. I thought it was the best day of my life, and I remembered how Mom laughed when I'd told her that, and I didn't understand why.

My mom used to sing me a lullaby...

I could feel her here now, with me. She was on the other side, waiting for me.

But my vision was going dark, and pure panic took over my mind until there were no words left. Until I hardly had a mind anymore to think with.

Death reached for me, but along with it came something warm and familiar. I could feel Mom. If this was death, I didn't have to be so scared anymore. I had no mind left, no body. Just the feeling of love on the other side.

And the darkness swallowed me whole.

CHAPTER 26—ORION

$\mathcal{I}$ knew I was dreaming, but I still felt as if she were right here before me. I could smell her in my dream, intoxicating.

She was standing on the coffee table in my living room, no longer in the thick woolen dress. Now, she wore a short black dress with long sleeves that puffed at the shoulders. A line of buttons ran down the front, and her red hair cascaded over the dark silk. She wore black stilettos.

My arms had been bound behind me with thick rope that chafed at my wrists...

Why was I dreaming about having my arms bound?

For a moment, I felt a strange sense of urgency, a desperation to rip free of them.

I was here now, with Rowan—or Mortana. If I could move, I could touch her. Taste her. She was only two feet away from me. If I could move my arms, I could pull her into my lap. I wanted to fuck her again, more than I'd ever wanted anything.

But that was a betrayal of Ashur and all the rest. I *owed* him revenge. There had to be, after all, a reason I'd survived when none of the others had. Why me, when I was the worst among them?

Because I could kill so easily—a brutal skill that I'd been born with. It was my one purpose. I must speak for the dead, to exact revenge when they no longer could. I was their voice and their sword. I would make the mortals pay.

I couldn't trust Rowan. And even if she'd changed— even if she was a new person completely—I was sure she would betray me.

But all those ideas were flying out of my head right now because Rowan was standing on the table in high heels, and I could not keep my eyes off her thighs.

I pulled my gaze up to stare at her lush red lips. How was it that her face looked innocent and sinful all at once? Her beauty overwhelmed me. It always had.

She took a step closer to me, heels clacking on the mahogany. "You know, Orion, I still remember your real name. From the old days. You were always so desperate to please me back then. I loved it when you begged."

She started to unbutton the top of her dress, and my blood pounded. Under the dress, she wore a red silk bra.

"What are you doing?" My voice came out husky and desperate.

She bit her lip coquettishly. "What I've always done. Tormenting you. I like the feeling of power I've got over you, Orion." Her dress was unbuttoned to her navel now, and I stood entranced as she opened it further, revealing sheer red underwear.

She let the dress drop to the floor. I swallowed hard as she stepped down off the coffee table, posing before me with a tantalizing bounce of her breasts.

She pulled down one strap of her bra. "Orion, I want you to tell me that I'm your queen. Don't you think I would make a better ruler than you?"

Her nipple was exposed—pink and hard—and I could no longer think straight. Queen…? I wanted her mouth wrapped around me.

She pulled down the other strap, and I desperately wanted her to untie me. My cock was now painfully hard.

Between us, the air felt charged with sexual desire. I fed from hers, just as she fed from mine. "I don't even want you, Rowan. Haven't I already told you that? I find you tedious."

Her gaze moved to my crotch, where the evidence of my mendacity was obvious. "Is that so?"

"Why don't you start by untying me?" I rasped. "And then we will negotiate what I will and will not agree to."

She stepped between my knees and straddled me, pressing her breasts against my chest. Her bare thighs were wrapped around my waist.

I was going to lose my mind. Perhaps it was already gone. Every muscle in my body was tense, coiled tight.

I exhaled a long, shuddering breath. *Stay in control,*

Orion. She was, of course, the same Mortana she'd always been.

Clenching her thighs around mine, she leaned back a little and started unbuttoning my shirt. "So much hate in you, Orion. Don't you think you would make a terrible king? Don't you think the world would be better off with you as my subject, seeing to my needs?" She pulled open the last button and stroked her hand down my chest. "Think about how much you'd truly love to submit to me…"

"Fuck, no." Right now, I wanted nothing more than to lie back and let her ride me. I ached to caress her, but for the sake of Ashur, I was denying myself what I wanted.

She unbuttoned my pants, fingers grazing against me.

I gasped, and she gave me a wicked smile. "Liar. I know what you want. I can feel it in the air, you know." Her fingers brushed against me again, and I gritted my teeth.

I will give almost anything if you use my body—

She looked down, then gave me a half smile. Leaning forward, she nestled her head into the crook of my neck. Her breasts pressed against my bare chest, and she trailed hot kisses over my skin. She moved her hips against me, and I groaned, no longer able to control myself. "Why don't you untie me, love?" I murmured. "And I'll give you what you need."

She brushed her lips against mine. "I think about you, Orion. Do you know, when I was near death, I thought of you? When the Malleus Daemoniorum nearly killed me,

I hungered for you. Because you know, Orion, for Lilu like us, sex isn't just sex. It's life."

She stood up again, giving me a full view of her sexy body, and tension coiled tight within me.

Sliding her hands into the sides of her underwear, she pulled them down slowly. *Fuck.* She was pure perfection, and my tongue ached to caress every inch of her skin, to lick her between her thighs…

When she straddled me again, I could tell she was as turned on as I was. Her hand slid between her legs, grazing my shaft as she moved it. I couldn't take my eyes off her, and my hips jerked against her. "Rowan," I moaned in desperation.

This was *agony*.

"I think about you when I'm turned on," she said breathlessly. "I always have."

It was, I realized, what I'd always wanted to hear, and my breath caught. I was the dead coming to life with electric currents—a painful process, but the only thing that would get my blood pumping once more. I needed to be inside her.

As my lust mingled with hers, I'd been feeding, gaining in strength, in the power of an incubus. The ropes strained against my wrists, and I pulled with all my might, ripping the strands and fibers of the bindings apart. Rowan leapt up, but I captured her in my arms.

I threw her down on my sofa and spread her thighs wide. She had a victorious sort of smile as I pinned her wrists above her head. At last, I slid into her, the pleasure overwhelming. She reached for my hair, threading her fingers into it. This wasn't just sex though, was it? We were connected. She was a part of me, the music of my life, and I needed her. Flames ignited in my heart.

"Rowan," I said huskily, "tell me you will never betray me."

"Orion," she whispered, "I thought about you when I died."

The embers in my chest snuffed out. My blood ran cold, and I stopped moving. "What did you just say?"

She touched the side of my face. "I thought about you when I died in the underworld. You know I'm not really here, right?"

* * *

I WOKE, my heart slamming against my ribs, and looked around my dark room. Loneliness pierced me, and my body felt cold. I tried to shake off the feeling of horror.

That was a dream though, wasn't it? She hadn't *actually* died.

Catching my breath, I touched my chest. My heartbeat felt sluggish and dull.

For the first time in ages, the embers in my heart lay dead.

Did I miss her that much?

I'd lived for one reason, and one reason alone: to act as the sword of the dead. To give them the revenge they wanted.

But something felt *wrong*, and I desperately wanted to see Rowan again.

CHAPTER 27—ORION

I sat on my balcony, sipping Syrah and trying to shake off the horror of my bad dream. Moonlight dappled the ocean with silver, and a warm, salty breeze rolled off the water. It was always magically warm here in the City of Thorns, a perfect temperature for my future kingdom.

Three in the morning was an absurd time to drink wine, but I hadn't been able to get back to sleep since I'd woken with my heart thundering. Something still felt *off* in the world. Unbalanced. Dread threaded through my veins.

Maybe the dream meant nothing, and it was just nerves for the impending regicide I had planned in a few hours. By dawn, I should be standing before the Tower of Baal's gates, holding the severed head of Cambriel, his blood dripping just below Nergal's head. The whole city would see the mark of Lucifer beaming from my forehead. They would all know their true king had arrived at last.

It wouldn't be long until my demon subjects would be ripping the mortals to shreds when I unleashed hell on Earth. I'd dreamed of this for centuries, ever since they'd marched me by my family's severed heads on the way to the prison.

So why the fuck did I feel such an overwhelming sense of dread?

I shifted in my chair, disturbed by the late-night quiet.

I lifted my glass of wine, watching the moonlight reflect off its dark surface. I suppose what bothered me was that I had no idea what Rowan was doing. But why would she delay her return here?

Maybe I needed to understand what she was.

I set the glass of wine on a table and went back into my library. Ka...a word from the ancient days, something buried deep under centuries of mundane memories.

From my bookshelf, I pulled out an old tome called *Book of the Dead*, its binding brown leather etched with gold letters. I dropped into a velvet armchair and flipped through the yellowed handwritten pages.

From a sconce behind me, candlelight wavered over the old book. It was written in an ancient demonic language that I could read, albeit slowly. I found a page with a strange drawing of a horned demon. Not quite horns, I supposed, but rather arms and hands jutting from his head.

My blood pounded harder as I read through the text.

According to this book, demons had souls like mortals did. And a soul wasn't just a spirit but comprised of several different aspects: the life-force (ka), the personality (ba), and the memories (ren).

When someone died, their ka left the body and became a double. The ka lived on—a sort of demonic doppelgänger in the world of the dead. Rowan, then, had somehow come from the doubleworld.

My heart leapt at the implication. If all this was true, then the original Mortana was dead.

And the real question at the heart of this was whether this made Rowan the same person as Montana.

Fucked if I knew. I wasn't a philosopher.

On the one hand, she was clearly different. She had different memories, different experiences to shape her life, a very different personality...all those aspects of her soul had changed. Rowan had chosen to save my life twice—once in Purgatory, and again in the forest. Letting me die would have solved all her problems, and all she'd have had to do was fail to act. Mortana would have left me to die, without a doubt.

Guilt clenched my chest. If she wasn't Mortana, I'd been cruel to her for no reason.

Then again, I had to find a way to keep myself away from her, no matter what. This new Rowan would try to pull me off my path. She'd never accept the revenge I craved.

I slammed the book shut and traced my fingers over its surface. Already, she was distracting me. I had a king to kill, and I needed to clear my head.

I prowled across the room for my collection of knives. This was all I would need to kill the king—daggers to slaughter the guards.

I strapped them to my waist, my thighs, loading myself up with blades.

Fully armed, I crossed out to the balcony. For a moment, I stood there, looking out over the dark sea. If things went according to plan, this would all be over soon. After everything that had happened to us, an incubus would be on the throne.

My wings shot out from my shoulder blades, kissed by the balmy ocean breeze. As they pounded the air, I took off into the dark night sky.

Now, I no longer cared if the whole city knew I was Lilu. Let them stare. They'd be kneeling before me soon.

Every one of them who'd stood by while the Lilu were slaughtered would be on their knees.

* * *

AT THE TOP of the Tower of Baal, the air thinned. I landed quietly on the balcony, the wind howling around me. No one bothered to lock a balcony door when it was over five thousand cubits high, piercing the night sky.

No one knew I could fly.

I pulled one of the knives from its sheath and slowly slid the balcony door open.

Silently, I moved over the black and white mosaic floor. With the moonlight streaming in, I could make out the contour of Cambriel sleeping next to someone in a bed with sea-blue blankets.

The enormous room was made of sharply peaked arches and columns of pale stone. Engravings of beautiful winged goddesses jutted from the tops of some of the columns, and the arches had been painted with constellations. Maybe the monarchs had killed my kind, but they still liked to use us as inspiration for art.

The air smelled faintly as if they'd just been having sex, which I didn't want to think about. Briny air rushed into the room, toying with the gauzy curtains.

Neither of them stirred as I quietly approached. The woman's presence was annoying, but I should be able to silence her easily enough. I pulled another knife from a sheath and threw it into the air. The blade found its mark, and the hilt jutted from the woman's throat. I'd severed her voice box, so she couldn't scream, and I rushed over to the bed before she could wake the king with her flailing. Up close now, I slit the king's throat. Blood sprayed over the bed.

This was how I had known that I was destined to rule: no one else could spend hundreds of years in a dungeon and emerge knowing exactly how to murder people with the precision and efficiency of a trained warrior. When Lucifer had marked me, he'd endowed me with unnatural gifts.

I pulled another knife out and crawled between the two demons as they bled onto their pillows. My claws elongated, and with a feral snarl, I ripped the king's heart from his chest.

I shoved his limp body out of the bed and lifted his blood-stained pillow.

Nothing lay beneath it.

What the *fuck*, Rowan?

The king started making a gurgling sound, already healing. This was the magic of the book, of course, because otherwise, he'd be dead without a heart. Had she lied?

I shoved the bleeding woman off the bed, and she dropped onto the tile floor with a thud. No book under her pillow, either.

My heart pounded like a war drum, and the king let out a strangled scream as he healed.

In the next heartbeat, two guards burst into the room, swords drawn. But a sword wasn't much use from across the room, which was why I had brought the knives. I pulled out two more and threw them with precision. They arced through the air, striking the guards in their hearts.

By now, Cambriel had regained the use of his vocal cords, and the idiot king was screaming like a child. I had to act quickly, before the rest of his army found their way upstairs and made this job significantly harder.

"Where's the book?" I asked quietly.

"What book?" he screamed, his voice mangled.

Of course he wasn't going to tell me.

"Rowan said it would be under your pillow."

"Who is Rowan?" he pleaded. "What book are you talking about?"

Right? Of course. He didn't know her by that name.

I pulled a knife from a strap at my waist and threw it hard. The blade pierced the top of his hand and pinned his palm to the floor. He screamed, agonized. I could torture him as long as was necessary to get the answers out of him, but I wouldn't have that long before I was fighting off an entire army.

"The book that keeps you alive," I said through gritted teeth. "Where is it?"

"There's no book!" he shrieked. "I don't have a magic book. What are you *talking* about? How did you get up here?"

I crossed closer to him and knelt between his legs. Pulling one of my last knives from its sheath, I slammed it through his thigh, close to his crotch. "The book, Cambriel."

"Someone lied to you." He inhaled, a deep, heaving sob, then laughed with an unnerving sort of hysteria. "Orion, I don't know how you got that star of Lucifer, but you aren't the true king any more than I am. Only Mortana was destined to rule. Why the fuck do you think I wanted to marry that maniac?"

"Nergal was my father. My mother was a Lilu," I said. "I am the king's true son. I should inherit the throne. That was how I could kill him."

"That's the thing." He clutched his thigh with his free hand, sweat pouring down his face. "Nergal really wasn't your father, nor mine. The old fucker was sterile. If your mother was Lilu, perhaps she didn't know who your father was at all." Wild laughter. "The Lilu whores had so many lovers, didn't they? I'm not trying to be rude, but you can't trust a succubus. And you can't trust Mortana. If she won't marry me, she must die." With his right hand, he ripped the blade out of his left. "We will kill her together. It's the only way. Don't you see? She will bring us both down."

I took a step back from him, quickly evaluating the situation. This mission must be aborted. My mind whirled...

"No. I will find out how to kill you, Cambriel," I said quietly.

He pulled the blade from his thigh and rose, shaking.

As he did, a guard burst into the room. And unfortunately for me, this one had a gun.

Everything next happened so fast.

Four bullets hit me in the chest. Pain shot through my body, and I staggered back. It was almost starting to feel like Rowan had set me up to get me out of the way...

I turned to head for the balcony. As I did, Cambriel rushed out before me, panicking. Bleeding, I hurried out after him. Another bullet slammed into my shoulder, and I nearly fell to my knees.

Cambriel panicked and threw himself off the balcony. Unlike me, he didn't have wings.

I peered over the edge, watching him plummet into the darkness. Unfortunately for me, he would recover.

My wings shot out of my shoulder blades, sending a sharp jolt of pain down my spine. But already, I was starting to heal.

I took off into the air, trying to think of a new strategy. My cover here was blown. I was back to square one when it came to killing the king, and my plans were unraveling.

I wondered if I should fly down to the king, pick up what was left of him, and interrogate him when he woke up. Maybe there'd be time to get to him before his soldiers identified the puddle of gore.

Circling overhead, I was overcome with a cold sense of dread. It was *too* quiet...

I'm not worried about you, love. You don't have it in you.

I'd issued a challenge to her, and that was starting to seem like a big mistake. And maybe I'd been wrong, because I hadn't imagined it would be possible for her to lie to me about the book. Nor had I expected her to pull a knife on me and kick me out of the underworld without her.

Alarms started ringing across the city, but they sounded dull to my ears. I soared over the ancient city of stone.

Right now, the only thing that seemed real to me was that horrible dream—Rowan telling me that she'd died. But if it wasn't real, why did I feel her absence like a tangible thing, like it was cold soil burying me?

Why did the world seem so silent, so frozen? This beautiful city had become a tomb—an enormous dungeon.

She was dead.

Ice settled in my veins. As much as I wanted to scrape up the king's remains, my mind was on Rowan.

An unfamiliar feeling—*fear*—crept over my skin.

What if Rowan *had* died beyond the veil? Maybe if I

hadn't been so hellbent on pushing her away, she'd be with me now.

You can't hate someone you don't respect.

Dread chilled my blood. I'd been an asshole.

I soared over the city gates and started to head for the world beyond the veil. It would take me days to get back to her, to get through Purgatory and find out what had happened, but I wasn't going to wait any longer.

CHAPTER 28—ROWAN

I opened my eyes, allowing them to adjust to the darkness. I lay on frozen earth. A grave, perhaps? A few rays of silver moonlight shone on the icicles hanging from the trees around me. Not buried underground, then.

It felt as though someone had ripped out my skeleton and shoved it back in my body.

My breath came out in icy puffs. The cold air stung my cheeks and hands, and my teeth chattered. I rolled over onto my side and pushed myself up. Would I see Mom here? My vision sharpened. I was still in the underworld, which I suppose made sense. After all, I *was* dead.

"Rowan." I jumped at the sound of my name and turned to see Tammuz, the Dying God. Star-flecked shadows slithered over his bronze skin. He took a few steps closer to me. "You've returned."

"Thanks for the help."

"I drew the mob here." He towered over me, unnaturally tall. "I thought you needed to die."

I was still on the ground, but I was too exhausted to stand. "Some might consider that insulting, you know."

"You needed to die," he said again, "so that I could bring you back to life again. It's the only way to stop you from fearing death."

I rose on unsteady feet. "You brought me back to life? So...I'm not dead? I can leave the underworld?"

I looked down. The dress was gone, and I was wearing leather pants, a shirt, and a warm coat with a black fur collar.

"You were right, Rowan," he said. "I want you to have a chance at the crown. It's no fun if Orion takes it without any competition, is it?"

He faded into the shadows and reappeared a few inches from me in a gust of cold wind. Reaching up, he touched my cheek. He had the same high cheekbones as Orion, the same sharp jaw. Thick black eyebrows. He was a god, tens of thousands of years old, but he looked no older than thirty.

"How did it feel?" he asked, his dark eyes gleaming with curiosity.

"Not great, Tammuz," I said. "Strangling to death is *not* my idea of a good time." I swallowed. "But at the end, I felt like I was heading to my mom." I waved a hand at my new duds. "How did I wind up in these clothes?"

"They grew with you from the earth." He held my gaze and nodded. "You were with your mother for thirteen hours."

My jaw dropped, and I felt a wild sort of excitement. "What? Why don't I remember it?"

"I can't allow you to remember it."

"Why not?"

"Because it's not a memory for the living," he said with finality.

"For the living..." I repeated, my thoughts slow and sluggish. But I'd recently died, so I wouldn't be too hard on myself.

His eyebrow arched. "Do you know, that's exactly how Mortana died? Your death played out the same way. You and she experienced the same death."

I rubbed my throat. "They kept yelling at me, saying that I'd sacrificed my kin to save myself. It was like they knew what had happened with my mom." I frowned. "I guess the same goes for Mortana. She sacrificed all the Lilu to save her own ass."

"In the double world," he said in a faraway voice, "people play out the same tragedies, again and again."

He stepped back on the frosted earth and lifted his right hand. Silver claws grew from his fingertips. Shimmering, he vanished and reappeared a few feet away. "Orion has almost no fear."

"Because he believes his soul died in the dungeon." I looked down at Tammuz's claws, and my heart clenched. "You're...uh...not going to kill me again, are you?"

"No. I am going to teach you to fight like a demon. You may die in the process, if you are not careful, but you will return again."

I raised my eyebrows. "That'll take a long time, I'm afraid. How long do we have?"

"Time passes differently in the doubleworld. We will take as long as we need. As my son, Orion inherited my ability to kill, but you will have to learn it."

I was going to fight with the Dying God in a frozen underworld. I waited for terror or a feeling of dread, but I'd already died and had nothing to fear anymore.

I lunged forward. Claws sprang from my fingertips, and I struck at Tammuz's chest, but I'd been too slow, hesitating at the last moment.

His claws ripped through me before I could take another breath.

*   *   *

USING A TREE BRANCH, I pulled myself up, feeling the ache in my muscles. The ice stung my fingers, and the cold air burned my lungs. I sucked in a deep breath and exhaled, sending billows of frosty mist floating among the crystalline branches.

I'd died four times so far, and I was starting to get used to it. Tammuz had a thing for killing me and bringing me back...when he wasn't finding ways to torture me with exercise and endless sparring. But truth be told, I was enjoying the physicality of our encounters. It helped me shut off my mind and forget the visions he'd given me.

But it also made me wildly hungry, and I was

surviving on acorns and berries, not the most satisfying of diets.

Tammuz materialized in the dark grove. "Enough. It's time for you to run."

I dropped out of the tree onto the snowy earth and did as the god commanded.

WITH MY WINGS OUT, I soared behind him over snow-frosted trees. His deep gold wings glowed, making him easy to follow through the night sky. The speed of our chase exhilarated me. We pitched and rolled though the marine winds.

The icy sea air tore through my hair, and I raced after Tammuz over the waves. I angled my wings like he did, curving back over the rocky shore.

A WINTER WIND whispered through the trees. The Dying God stood behind me. Placing his hands on my hips, he shifted my stance slightly.

"Bend your legs more," he said. "Swing your torso, twist your hips, and use your whole body."

I obeyed, punching the air slowly, trying to perfect my form.

"Good. Faster."

My fist shot out, lightning-quick.

He disappeared, materializing again in front of me. I aimed for his jaw, but he blocked it.

* * *

FINALLY, I landed a punch to his temple, my knuckles stinging with the force of the blow.

His response was swift and brutal. Pressing his right forearm against my throat, Tammuz crushed me against a tree trunk. I stared into his dark, forest-green eyes. Pain pierced me, a momentary shock, and then his claws ripped my ribs apart, and darkness fell.

* * *

FROM THE GROUND, Tammuz swept at my feet, scissoring his legs. I spread my wings and rose into the air. Snapping my wings shut, I dropped, landing on his ribs, and slammed my fist into his face.

Something caught my eye—a dark rock covered in snow. It reminded me of chocolate cake. Hunger was driving me mad.

He flung me aside, sending me crashing into a tree. Leaping to his feet, he darted into the woods. I followed close at his heels, dodging tree branches.

* * *

AFTER MONTHS of training with Tammuz, I'd grown infinitely stronger, but also hungry as fuck. There was no pizza here in the underworld, no ice cream.

Each day, I slept in the cottage with the warm fire and the bearskin rug. Tammuz had given me a gift—my demonic magic had returned. But he didn't seem to eat, so I was on my own in that regard. The thought of clam chowder from the inn was tempting, but if I left the forest, I'd be hanged before I had time to enjoy the first bite.

My stomach ached as I wandered back to the cabin, looking for anything I could forage along the way. Sometimes, I gathered mushrooms, juniper berries, acorns, cranberries, and wintergreen for tea.

The sun was up, and tangerine light spread over the snow. It *looked* good enough to eat, sweet and fruity, like Italian ice.

In the morning light, a splash of ivory caught my eye. My stomach rumbled. A large cluster of oyster mushrooms sprouted from a log across a snowy clearing. Ravenous, I hurried over and ripped them from the log, shoving them into my little leather bag. I knew from experience that they tasted better cooked. As much as I wanted to gobble them raw, I'd wait and fry them in an iron pan back at the cabin.

Unfortunately, mushrooms had almost no calories. Kneeling on the icy ground, I foraged every bit of the fungus, soaking the knees of my pants in the wet snow.

The forest was my guide and the key to my survival, telling me what to eat and where to find it. I knew, for instance, that the white mushrooms that sprang up behind Tammuz were toxic and would make me vomit for days.

Goosebumps rose on my skin. The forest was speaking to me. I looked up from the log, the faint sound of moving water catching my attention. A stream I hadn't yet discovered.

Lured by the promise of food, I started running, kicking up snow behind me. The forest didn't disappoint. Water swirled between rocks, and rainbow trout slowly swam in a pool.

My claws came out, my mouth already watering. Ignoring the freezing cold, I waded in to catch my dinner.

* * *

A HEAVY SNOW fell around us. For the first time, I was training with a full belly, and I felt strong. Tammuz swiped at me, claws out, and I dodged him. Momentum brought his head down, and I punched him twice, exactly like he'd taught me.

As he recovered, I thought I saw a faint smile.

* * *

WRAPPED in a blanket before the hearth, I soaked my feet in warm water, muscles burning, and slowly ate a piece of venison jerky. Months of endless winter had passed. Maybe a year.

After the great trout discovery, I'd grown strong and fast enough to hunt deer with a knife. For the past two months, meat had been on the menu.

Chewing, I leaned back and let my calves soak in the warm water. Outside, the sun was starting to set.

The passage of time here confused me, and it didn't help that I'd died so many times. After the initial hanging, at least all the deaths Tammuz delivered had been mercifully quick. Each time he'd ripped my heart out, death had come too soon for me to register the pain. So far, I hadn't managed to return the favor, not once.

Each time he killed me, I awakened surrounded by snow and bone-white mushrooms and the vague impression that I'd seen Mom again.

Each time, I was wearing a brand-new warrior's outfit.

All night, I ran and sparred. I built my muscles. I learned to hit and kick and bring out my claws. I died, again and again. I learned to summon fire, to unleash my wings. Over and over, I practiced, using my demonic strength and sense of balance in ways that mortals could not. I leapt high, swinging from branches. I learned how to inflict damage with my elbows and how to hover in the air to kick.

Sometimes, when the Dying God had a blade to my throat and the shadows whipped around him, I'd feel the familiar sting of fear, but it wasn't the same, not like it once had been.

I'd learned. I knew now that it would all be over, and fast.

I returned from being dead again and again. The old terror no longer clung to me, sliding away like pasta coated in oil.

I finished the jerky and picked up my mug of hot pine needle tea. The steam swirled around me. Soon, I'd be asleep on the floor. Every time I curled up on the bear skin rug, I'd think of Orion and the first time we'd come here. And that was how I drifted off to sleep each morning.

A lonely sort of peace had found me in this cabin and quiet isolation.

Only one thing troubled me now: did I have it in me to take Orion down?

What if the only way to stop him was to kill him, but I couldn't bring myself to do it?

CHAPTER 29—ROWAN

*T*he months stretched on, and my patience with the Dying God wore thin. I stood across from him in the clearing, ice daggers glittering from the tree branches around us. I felt infinitely stronger now than I once had, ready to take on anything, but he still didn't think I was ready.

Snowflakes drifted around us, sparkling in the moonlight. Dark, smoky magic twined around him, a tunic of shadows against his bronzed skin.

Tammuz moved in a blur of speed, but I was ready for him this time. I'd learned through painful trial and error that you couldn't simply lunge for a demon's heart—he'd find a way to protect it, pivoting away on instinct. I'd felt the same impulse every time Tammuz had darted toward me, and I'd turn, taking his claws in my shoulder or back. Anything but the heart, and a demon would be fine, recovering almost instantly. So when Tammuz wanted to kill me, he'd beat the shit out of me first, raining blows and punches to my head, until my reflexes slowed and I staggered, forgetting to shield.

While I wasn't so scared of death anymore, I was done with getting hit in the head. And the loneliness cut me down to my bones.

"Tammuz," I said, "you've got to let me go at some point."

Snow fell on his bare shoulders and arms and melted into glistening droplets. "No."

I sighed. "Are you lonely? Is that it?" I knew why he was keeping me here. It was no fun for the god of chaos if I didn't stand a chance in the fight for the throne, but I was tired of being controlled.

He faded into the shadows and appeared behind me. "You don't fight like you want to kill yet, Rowan. You fight like it's your hobby. You need to connect with your rage."

I didn't want to kill Orion, but maybe that wasn't who I needed to think about when I fought.

I closed my eyes, envisioning my half brother, Cambriel, hunting Mom through the woods. I pictured him unleashing an arc of fire on her. She'd burned to death trying to protect me.

Ice-cold rage slid through my veins. I turned to face the Dying God, but Tammuz had changed. He'd trans-formed into the false king, his dark hair lightened to pale blond. A golden crown rested on his head.

Cambriel. I hated that arrogant prick.

This was what I'd dedicated my life to—revenge. And finally, I was strong enough to make it mine.

He'd killed my whole family, all because he was desperate to stay on a throne he never deserved.

Fury cracked through my body like lightning. As he moved forward, swinging a punch at me, I grabbed his arm, blocking the blow, and slammed my other hand into his trapped arm. A bone cracked, and Cambriel grunted in pain.

Kill. The word blazed through my mind. *Kill.*

I leapt into the air, gripped a tree branch, and kicked him hard in the jaw. He flew backward into a trunk.

By the time I descended, he'd already recovered. He lashed out at my head, but I ducked. I straightened and sent another hard blow to his jaw, then a fast left hook. His head snapped back, but he landed the next punch. The blow dizzied me for a moment. I regained my footing and flew into the air, wings spreading out behind me. As I plummeted, I brought my heel down hard onto his head. The force of the kick slammed him into the frozen earth. Angling my wings, I dove for him, claws gleaming.

I came down on his chest, and Cambriel's dark eyes opened wide in surprise. Hungry for vengeance, I carved his heart from his chest with my claws. I caught my breath. Blood dripped from my hands onto the snow. Never in my life had I felt so much like a wild beast.

As I stared at the body, it transformed back into Tammuz—his skin and hair darker now, his arms bare. He was completely naked.

I held the heart of a god in my hands and watched him die, the life fading from his dark eyes. Panic gripped me, but then I remembered that Tammuz did this all the time.

My claws retracted, and I dropped his heart on the ground. Smoke swept around him, and his body disappeared, leaving bloodstains behind in the snow. I sat to catch my breath, trying not to think about what had happened.

I'd just been sitting on Orion's naked dad.

My body raced with adrenaline. So *that* was what it felt like to be a hunter—to be a demon. I stared down at my bloody palms, then wiped them clean on the snow, washing the god's blood from my hands as best I could.

Leaning back against a tree trunk, I waited for Tammuz to return. The loneliness of the quiet forest pierced me. For what had felt like ages, I'd been nothing but a warrior. Tammuz wasn't the best company.

Slowly, a circle of ivory mushrooms pushed through the snow—Destroying Angels, they were called. Maybe that was what I'd become.

Then the Dying God sprouted from the earth like a plant. He was lying on his back, his hair spread out around him. Smoke snaked around his powerful body, and his dark tattoos slid into place.

Fully formed, he opened his eyes and sat up, breathing in deeply. He rose to his full height, his expression bemused. He glanced to the east, toward the ocean where the morning sun was starting to rise.

I got to my feet, brushing the snow off my clothes. Exhaustion pulled at me. "Glad to see you back, Tammuz."

"No, you're not." His voice echoed around me in a deep chorus. "Go to sleep, Rowan. Rest. At nightfall, you will leave." He met my gaze. "It's time for you to kill the false king."

Joy leapt in my heart.

Finally, I was ready. I would take down the monster who'd killed my mom.

And I hoped Orion didn't get in my way.

I AWOKE in the early evening, my normal circadian rhythm now fully backward, and prepared to leave the forest for what seemed like the first time in a year. Readying for my departure, I dressed in one of the outfits Tammuz had given me, tight black leather pants and a shirt, and a dark cape around my shoulders.

As I walked through the forest, the sun was starting to set, spreading across the sky in lurid shades of pumpkin and honey. Night had fully descended by the time I reached the old Walcott Street.

Since I had no interest in hanging again or getting attacked by a mob, I quickly headed for the coastline, reminding myself that only a few hours had passed in the rest of the underworld. If anyone caught sight of me, they'd realize I was no longer hanging at the end of a rope where I should be.

Dark waves churned and crashed against the rocky shoreline. Under the ebony sky, the sea frothed and foamed on slick rocks. Hiding my face in the hood of the cloak, I hurried along the coast, the briny wind whipping at me, following a salty tributary toward Salem Village. Heron stood along the edge of the river, and I wondered what they'd done to end up here. A strange little hut of twigs and dried mud had been built by the riverside. *Wattle and daub*, I thought. It had a thatched roof with a rough clay chimney, and smoke curled into the darkening sky. A strange, witchy little place.

I kept my face covered as I hurried along, but just as I scurried past the door, I heard someone call my name and went still.

"Rowan?" The voice was familiar. Familiar and loved...

My heart sped up as a woman poked her head out of the hut.

Shai's hair hung in beautiful black ringlets around her head. She was dressed in a gray dress with a wide white collar. I stared at her, stunned.

"Shai?"

She hurried over to me and grabbed me by the arms. "Are you really here? Oh, my God. Rowan?"

"Are *you* really here?" I was too shocked to say anything else.

"How long have we been stuck here?" she asked. "It feels like a week."

I shook my head. "I think time flows differently for you and me. I've been here a year."

Her eyes widened, and she gripped my arm more tightly. "*What?*"

"I don't understand," I said. "How did you end up

here? I thought only demons could go beyond the veil, and mortals who—" I froze. "Mortals who died."

Her smile faltered, and she let go of my arm. "I don't think I'm dead. I'd know if I was dead, right?"

No one else here seemed to realize they were dead. With a lump in my throat, I asked, "What do you remember about how you got here?"

"The car disappeared as we were driving. Then I landed hard by a frozen forest. Oh, and there were caves…Rowan, I don't think I'm dead."

I swallowed hard. "It sounds like how I got here." I took her by the hand. "Let's see if we can get you out of here. Maybe you're part demon. Do you think you could be?"

She held out her hand, wiggling her fingers. "My mom said we were part Luciferian on her father's side, but I never knew if it was true. Maybe that's why I'm so good at animal healing magic, don't you think? I've always been at the top of my class. Magic comes naturally to me."

I glanced at the hut. "But how have you survived here?"

She heaved a deep sigh. "I've been healing sick cows. Someone let me use their old hut in exchange for helping their herd. They really value cows here. And goats. I need to get the fuck out of here before they realize what I am and hang me."

I took her hand and dragged her along the shore. "I can show you how to get back."

"Rowan, I cannot begin to tell you how happy I am that you found me. These people freak me the fuck out."

"Trust me," I said, "I know. I've already been hanged once."

"*What?*"

"Oh, it's okay. I got better. Think of it as a training exercise. The Dying God has taught me how to kill a king."

"Did you go insane here?"

"Come on, Shai. I'll explain along the way."

CHAPTER 30—ORION

I slid my hands into the pockets of my coat as I stalked the streets of Salem. Night had fallen by the time I reached the town center, and the dark sea battered the shore nearby. My lips tasted of salt. Orange lights punctuated the wooden buildings around me, and inside, people were dining by roaring fires. The air smelled of roasting meat. Apart from the people, the underworld wasn't really that bad.

If I breathed deeply, I could almost smell her floral scent here. Back in the City of Thorns, I'd been certain that Rowan was dead. Now, in the world of the dead, hope smoldered in my chest, and I felt myself coming to life again.

The sea wind stung my face, sharpening my senses—and I reminded myself how dangerous it was to hope. Was Rowan near?

Mortana had just been harping on that in Purgatory.

Every time I came through that bloody cave, it was worse than the time before.

As I walked past the House of Seven Gables, with its flickering orange windows inset into black wood, the memory of Purgatory still haunted my thoughts.

I'd seen Mortana holding my mother's heart in her hand. In the vision, she'd laughed at me, a wild sound that had echoed off the dungeon walls. My mother's corpse hung behind her on a rope from the dungeon ceiling, and Ashur's emaciated body lay at her feet. Behind her, heads on pikes cast shadows on the walls.

"You had a single purpose—to avenge those you loved. You *promised* Ashur you would take revenge on the mortals. You said you would kill me," Mortana had exulted. "But what did you do instead? You fell for me again. And I have deceived you, of course. Haven't you learned how stupid it is to hope? You were an idiot to trust me. I thought I'd taught you that lesson well. Looks like I need to try harder. I lied to you, and I'm coming for your throne now, Orion."

I shook my head, banishing her from my thoughts, and glanced at the stocks. A different woman hung in them today, her hair filthy with mud. She looked at me with piteous eyes. For a moment, I thought of breaking the wood to set her free, but if I did that, she'd likely be hanged as a witch.

To the left, Goody Putnam's tavern glowed with warmth and light. I peered inside, hoping to see Rowan's beautiful shock of red hair.

My heart fell when I spied Goody Putnam through

the windowpane, her cheeks flushed. I turned away and started for the Osborne Woods.

I'd taken but a few steps when Goody Putnam called after me. "Goodman Ashur," she shouted.

I turned to see her, pale hands clasped together, eyes gleaming with insane light. "Goodman Ashur, I am so very aggrieved to hear what happened to your wife."

I felt as if she'd shoved a blade into my chest.

"My wife," I repeated, hoping she'd fucking elaborate.

"Such an evil affair," she said, stepping closer to me. "She seemed familiar the first time I saw her. A creature from a nightmare. A most foul creature. She was caught in the woods with the devil last night."

I swallowed hard, torn between my need to hear more and the overwhelming desire to bash Goody Putnam's head against a wall. "Where is she now?"

The corner of her mouth twitched, and she licked her lips. "I have told everyone here that you must not have known—that you are a good man. But your wife was a witch. A demon. Judge Corwin hanged her on Gallows Hill as dawn broke."

The world shifted beneath my feet, and darkness swallowed me. This was my fault for pushing her away.

I gripped the woman by her shoulders. "Is she still there?"

"My husband died years ago, Goodman, and I have often hoped—"

I shoved her away from me and started for Gallows Hill, certain that my heart was breaking.

* * *

I DIDN'T FIND her hanging from the tree—just four rotting strangers. And that most dangerous thing, hope, returned. Maybe Goody Putnam was mad. I wandered into the darkening forest, hoping to find Rowan, or at least Tammuz.

Tammuz might have a clue what was going on.

As I trudged over the snowy earth, clouds slid across the moon. We had been together here recently, but somehow, it felt like ages past.

I glimpsed the little cabin in the forest, webs of frost icing the glass. Pushing open the door, I stepped inside.

Without a doubt, I could smell her here, and the place looked different than it had two nights ago. Strips of meat dried by the fire, and baskets of berries sat on the hearth. Women's clothes, clothes that were *her* size, had been folded and set aside. Candles had burned halfway down.

The cottage looked lived in.

I crossed to the sofa and lifted a blanket to my nose. Rowan. *Recently.*

My heart slamming against my ribs, I left the cabin and walked back into the forest. No summons was needed this time. Tammuz stood in the moonlight, his face illuminated with silver and his body cloaked in darkness.

"Where is she?" I rasped.

"Mortana? Dead."

"No, Rowan. She's different." I heard the wild desperation in my voice. "Where is she?" Snow swirled in wild vortices around us, and the night felt sharp with danger.

He shifted closer, the edges of his form blurring. "Ah, but you see, she lied to you. She didn't tell you how to kill the False King. She is after your crown, Orion. She aims to rule, to take what is yours." His eyes glittered. "Orion, don't you know that you should never let yourself hope?"

I stared at him, my heart twisting. Without the crown, everything I'd ever planned would be doomed. I was alive for one reason: to fulfill my oath to the dead and feed the earth with the blood of their enemies.

Tammuz blended into the night again.

I waited for the familiar anger to sizzle in my veins, rage at the knowledge that Rowan had lied to me.

But the anger did not come. We were doing as our destinies commanded, and nothing more. She had her fate, and I had mine. Like the sea crashing against the rocks, we could not escape the forces pulling at us. We were all alone, weren't we?

She would try to take the crown from me.

And I would make sure she failed.

CHAPTER 31—ROWAN

I crouched on the outer wall of the City of Thorns, gazing up at the Tower of Baal disappearing into the clouds.

I'd left my cloak with Shai so it wouldn't trip me up when I tried to kill the king. To our great mutual relief, Shai wasn't dead. She was in an Osborne hotel room, asleep.

If the rest of this night went the way I hoped, she'd be back here for my coronation when the sun was up.

Did I want to be queen?

Hell, yes.

I breathed in the perfumed, humid air of the City of Thorns. I belonged here. Outside the gates of this city, I was nothing. Broke, lonely, hunted by the mortal police. Vulnerable.

Out there, I'd end up in jail, eating cold macaroni off a tray and trying not to get the shit kicked out of me by people who thought I was a weirdo.

What would it be like to have some fucking respect for once? What would it feel like to have other people listen to me?

Hell, yes, I wanted all that. I'd never hungered for power before. I'd never dared to. It had seemed out of my reach.

But I hungered for it now. If that was the only way to keep myself safe, I wanted it.

Excitement fluttered through my heart as I pictured myself wearing a crown, stalking through the city. Deep down in my id, maybe a part of me admired Mortana. Not her sadism, but her willingness to take what she wanted. She wasn't afraid to be strong.

I didn't have many weapons—just two daggers strapped to my thighs—but my magic would do most of the work.

From here, I could see what appeared to be the entire demonic army stationed outside the tower—a legion of armed demons, horns and weapons glinting under the moonlight. Demons had never adapted well to guns, which they considered a vulgar mortal invention. They had too much pride to rely on weapons that powerful. Unfortunately, they did have arrows.

Still, no wonder they'd wanted the Lilu dead. Our wings gave us an extreme advantage over the rest of them. And when you added fire to the equation, I was a dangerous weapon.

As soon as I launched off this wall, they'd be sounding the alarms, the army rushing upstairs to protect the king.

They'd be looking for a Lilu, then, soaring through the skies.

Four guards stood outside a balcony window in the Tower of Baal. If I had to guess, that was where the king was sleeping. And if he was paranoid enough to station guards out there, he'd probably have powerful locks, alarms, reinforced glass...the hallways and stairwells outside his room would be packed with soldiers as well.

Were they well versed in fire safety? I doubted it.

My throat tightened. This was going to be messy and painful for everyone involved.

But if I was going to be queen, I couldn't alienate my future army by killing their friends. Whatever happened, I had to make sure the only person who died tonight was the fucker who'd killed my parents. Luckily, it was incredibly hard to kill a demon, so there shouldn't be any accidental deaths.

I hoped.

I cocked my head, staring from my perch on the windy tower wall at the army amassed at the base of the tower. They were everywhere. They hadn't swarmed the place like this when I'd been here before, so what had changed?

Orion.

I pieced it together. Of course. He'd entered the king's chambers, searching for the book I'd lied about. Guilt coiled in my chest. I hoped he hadn't been captured. But he'd made it *very* clear that I was on my own.

I glanced behind me, searching the skies for signs of

him, as if he might swoop in at the last moment and ruin my plans. Only the constellations gleamed above me.

At my best guess, it was around five-thirty a.m. Apart from the army, the whole city was asleep, windows darkened in stone buildings but for a sprinkle of lights. The sun would be rising soon, and with any luck, people would wake to the sight of me ripping out Cambriel's heart. Proof I was destined to lead.

With that glorious thought in mind, I took off from the parapet, soaring under the stars. The night wind rushed over me, skimming through my hair and feathers. Around the Tower of Baal, the soldiers shouted and stirred in alarm. A great bell tolled, echoing off the stones.

On the one hand, that was unfortunate. If Orion was anywhere nearby, the noise would alert him to my attack. What's more, the king would have time to prepare. On the other hand, I wanted the city awake. I needed an audience when I eviscerated their king.

Arrows flew through the air, and I picked up speed, climbing higher and out of their reach.

My gaze locked on a spot a few stories down from where the king slept, a balcony open to the air, an arch of stones overlooking the sea. I angled my wings and swept to a landing. Leaving the balcony, I crossed into a ballroom painted with murals of beautiful, winged Lilu. A golden light glowed in the deep blue marble floor. My five-pointed star had appeared.

Roughly a dozen soldiers in royal blue rushed at me, swords drawn. I folded my wings and lifted my hands, summoning the heat. It crackled in my chest, surging down my shoulders, arms, and wrists, and I unleashed a stream of fire in a protective arc around me. No one could walk through those flames without burning.

What would Mortana say at a time like this?

"Do you see my mark?" I shouted, my voice ringing in the marble hall. "I was made to rule. If you defy me, you will burn. And you should know that the king who sleeps in his room is a false king."

The soldiers stumbled back to avoid the fire. Regrouping, they pelted me with arrows. I ducked, but an arrow hit me in the shoulder, ripping through my muscle. I fell to my knees.

Just as Tammuz had taught me, I blocked out the pain and stayed on the offensive. From my knees, I let out another stream of fire. In the ensuing confusion, no one could aim properly. Gritting my teeth, I broke the arrow in half and ripped it out of my shoulder, grimacing as it tore my muscle. As soon as it was out, the wound began to heal.

I got to my feet and pressed on, fire streaming from my hands. Bright orange flames lit the darkness, warm light that danced over beautifully carved statues. Screams echoed from the tower's interior, and chaos reigned. People were alight, uniforms burning. They tumbled from the balcony, screaming on the way down. In the tower, balconies overlooked a fire pit far below, and curving stairways led between the floors. Shouting, the soldiers rushed to get away from me, fleeing the heat.

As I opened my wings to take flight to the top floor,

another arrow pierced my bicep, hitting bone. Pain sent a shockwave through me. *Block it out, Rowan.*

Glancing up, I saw the archer above me. He was protecting the king's door. I blocked out the noise and confusion, and summoned the calm of the forest.

Taking aim, I unleashed a stream of fire at the upper story. The blazing archer screamed and dropped his weapon. Behind him, the closely packed group of soldiers caught fire and leapt off the balcony to douse the flames, like breath blowing out a birthday candle.

I yanked the arrow out, blood spilling onto the floor. I'd better make this quick before they riddled me with arrows. I'd been focusing on the archer, and the protective ring of fire around me had dwindled. A swordsman lunged at me, and I sidestepped. Grabbing his wrist as I'd practiced so many times with Tammuz, I slammed his hands hard into the stone balcony, and he dropped his weapon.

My wings unfurled, and I took to the air, soaring to the top of the tower. Cool starlight streamed in through an oculus. Soldiers gathered outside the king's door, swords ready. The alarms were maddeningly loud, making it hard to think.

My heart was pounding hard, my body buzzing with adrenaline. Why wasn't Orion here, trying to stop me?

A soldier loosed an arrow at me, but his hands were shaking, and it went wide.

"Go!" My voice boomed over the tower. "You can see by the mark I bear that I am your queen."

"Not while the king still lives!" another shouted. "Only his heir can kill him. And he has no heir."

Two more arrows skimmed past my head.

I held up my hands. Fire crackled along my arms and danced from my fingertips. "Cambriel is not the true king. You will understand when you see his heartless corpse lying in your streets."

They were good soldiers, and they weren't moving from his door.

One of the archers took aim, and the arrow he fired struck me in the ribs. Agony slammed into me. I was fairly certain he'd punctured one of my lungs.

I sucked in a ragged breath and launched a stream of fire above their heads. Not close enough to burn them, but enough to make them panic. With the heat pressing down on them, the soldiers fled, a mad press of terrified men pushing and shoving their way down the stairs. In their haste, a few tumbled over the edge, plummeting to the lobby far below.

Clenching my jaws, I ripped the arrow out of my chest. The pain was exquisite. It would subside quickly, but for the moment, it was blinding, and I rasped for breath.

At last, I had a clear shot at the king's door—thick wood, reinforced with iron crosses and locked with an iron bar. My wings beat rhythmically behind me, pounding like my heart. I raised my hands and pointed at the door.

Hot magic sizzled through me, an inferno of heat that

poured out of me. In my mind's eye, I saw my mother's death, her last agonized moments.

I was an angel of destruction.

Cambriel had put me through hell. I would do the same to him.

CHAPTER 32—ROWAN

The door to the king's chamber caught fire, and the iron bars started to melt. The air smelled of seared wood and flesh.

The Tower was a pandemonium of shouting and fleeing, but I focused my attention on that burning door and the melting iron. Finally, the bar warped and slid to the stone floor in a puddle.

I swept through the fiery goo and into a great arched room. Three soldiers charged forward, surrounding me. One threw a punch, but I blocked it with my forearm. The force of his punch was crushing, and I heard the crack of bone.

The next one aimed for my head. Grabbing his wrist, I twisted it behind his back and spun him around to act like a shield.

I pivoted, placing his two companions between me and the door. The man I held captive elbowed me in the ribs with his free arm. His aim was either good or lucky, because he hit me in the *exact* spot where I'd just been pierced by an arrow. Pain shot through me, and fire exploded from my body. The man in my grip burst into flame, and the remaining two soldiers ran for the door. The fire spread, igniting the furniture and a tapestry on the wall.

I tossed the burned man aside and touched my ribs, wincing a little.

Cambriel stood alone in the center of the room, his face illuminated by the flames around him. His pale hair glowed orange in the light.

The wind rushed in through the open balcony, fanning the flames and tossing fiery sparks up to the high ceiling.

When I was queen, I would install fire sprinklers, because this place was absolutely *not* up to code.

Cambriel seemed unfazed, but he had no reason to fear fire. I turned quickly, unleashing another blast of fire at the door and locking us in together with a barrier of flames.

I took a step closer to him. "Cambriel. I saw what you did to my mother." I could hardly hide the fury in my voice.

He let out a short laugh. "How did you see *that*?"

"What happened between you two?" I demanded.

He placed a finger over his lips. "Do you know, Mortana, I don't really feel compelled to tell you. You can burn my army, if you want, but you cannot kill me. You're not my heir."

Hot anger churned in the depths of my chest. "You're

not the true king. You didn't kill Nergal. Tell me how you ended up lighting my mother on fire."

In a blur of speed, he rushed forward and clamped his hand around my throat, lifting me into the air. "Are you pretending that you care what happened to your mother? You left her for dead, Mortana, along with all the other Lilu. You don't give a fuck what happened to any of them. But I was willing to overlook your ruthlessness. We could have joined forces if you weren't so insane."

I kicked him hard in the chest, and he dropped me.

I just wanted the answer to one question before I ripped out his heart. "What did my parents want from you?"

"What difference does it make? Obviously, you have designs on the throne. That's why you're here, isn't it? I could have given it to you through marriage. Together, we could have been powerful."

I clenched my fists. "You are my half brother, *and* you murdered my parents."

He took a swing for me, but I blocked it, landing a hard punch in his stomach.

He doubled over, clutching his gut. "I don't know why you sound so put out. You ripped out my mother's heart and left her carcass in a vat of wine." He straightened. "But why all the questions about your parents? Are you lonely, Mortana, after you murdered the rest of your kind and left them to rot in the dungeons? I thought you wanted to be the only one left with your power. That's why you did it, isn't it? To gain power and save your own skin. You sacrificed your kin."

My fingers twitched. There was that phrase again—Mortana's original sin, and mine.

As soon as the fires died down behind me, more soldiers would swarm in. My wings shot out from my shoulder blades, lifting me into the air. I kicked Cambriel in the head, and he fell backward onto the floor.

He leapt up and exploded with flames. A fireball engulfed me. Orange and red danced around me, scented of ash and burning cloth. This was how Mom died. Cambriel relied on fire in a fight, a tactic that would work on almost anyone.

Except me. I didn't burn.

When the fireball receded, I angled my wings and slammed down on top of him, knocking him back to the floor. His head cracked against the stone. I straddled his waist, my long, silver claws extended. Bringing them down, I slashed his right wrist, severing his hand with the ring.

He shrieked in terror and grabbed my hair with his good hand. I could have ended his life right then and there by ripping out his heart, but I wanted an audience.

I raked my claws over his heart, threatening to pierce it, and drew a dagger from its sheath.

"My parents were blackmailing you," I snarled. "Why? What did they want?"

His eyes wide with fear, he shook his head wordlessly.

I poked his chest with my claws, drawing blood. "I watched her burn to death, Cambriel. Tell me what she wanted from you."

"Something I couldn't give. They wanted to come

back. I don't know why they suddenly had a sense of urgency after all those years."

Because I'd been born. This was my home, and they were trying to keep me safe.

"And why didn't you let them?" I roared. "He was your father, too."

His forehead glowed with his mark—a golden eye in a triangle. "And what if there were more? There was a reason the Lilu had to go. Nergal agreed to the mortals' demands because he wanted you gone, all of you. How can a wingless king rule over those who can fly? It was fine if you were the last one. You and I could marry. Our claims to the throne would be stronger than any others."

The fire had spread across the room, engulfing his bed.

His severed hand was already starting to heal, and I was out of time. I had the answer I needed.

I plunged the dagger into his heart. He froze, eyes wide. He'd be incapacitated until I got him out in a public square.

His words still rang in the hollows of my mind. *But what if there were more?*

I slid off his unconscious body and crouched to pick him up. I'd carry him through the window and—

A figure loomed in the burning doorway, someone impervious to the flames around him.

Orion. Coppery light and shadows danced over his features. Embers and smoke swirled around him, and his ice-cold eyes pierced the gloom. The scent of burning mahogany and heated stone filled the air, and ashes rained around the room.

The promise of violence hung thick in the air. "Well, Rowan. It would seem you found a way to break the blood oath and lie to me." He smiled. "But maybe I need to thank you. You've already done the hard work for me."

I wasn't here to have a dialogue with Orion, nor would I allow him to steal this chance from me. I wouldn't let him get in my head.

With the king in my arms, I raced for the open balcony door. Outside, the first blush of dawn spread over the demon sky, staining it a pearly coral.

When I reached the balcony, I would let my wings out—

A force like a train crashed into me from behind, knocking the wind from me before I could escape. I dropped the king, and we tumbled to the mosaic floor. I pushed onto my elbow and round kicked Orion in the knee.

He staggered, and I leapt to my feet, delighted by his surprised expression.

He wanted to fight? Fine. This is what I'd trained for. I widened my stance and cleared my head, calming my thoughts as the Dying God had taught me. Watching for signs of what my enemy would do next without emotion or fear.

I expected Orion to look furious, but he seemed amused instead. "Well, well," he said, the corners of his lips curling. "You *do* remember how to fight after all."

Smoke filled the air as the flames engulfed the furniture. "I learned a few things in the underworld."

"You want power for yourself."

I returned his faint smile. "When was the last time a queen ruled here instead of a king? And look at what angry men do when they have power. We saw it in the underworld. Men run that city. Women are hanged, put in stocks, and whipped, all because men can't bear the thought of women having the tiniest bit of control."

He arched an eyebrow. "So it's not for your own sake? You're doing this for all of womankind?"

"Forgive me for thinking it's a little unethical to slaughter all the mortals because someone pissed *you* off four hundred years ago."

His smile faded, and his eyes turned to ice. "Someone pissed me off? That's how you're describing it?"

"And yes, I do want to rule," I shouted. "So what? Maybe I'm sick of being pushed around by broken people on power trips."

He gave me a knowing smile. "And that's exactly what you would be, isn't it, a broken woman with half a soul on a power trip? I saw what you did to those soldiers burning outside—"

"They'll recover."

"The moment you learn how to use your magic, you start lighting people on fire and throwing them off balconies. Tell me how you're different from Mortana, again? You're already fighting just like her."

A sharp coil of doubt started to wind through my

thoughts. What was I doing? I was letting him get in my head.

Tammuz hadn't trained me for that, and if I listened to this too long, I would lose.

I needed to end this conversation before he completely got the upper hand. I shifted forward, ready to land a punch, but he swung for me first. Lightning fast, I ducked, then came up again with my claws aimed at his throat. He grabbed my wrists, pushing them out of the way, and slamming me onto the floor. I rolled, looking up at him from the ground.

Smoke billowed around me from a flaming chair at my side. Alarm bells clanged loudly in the city, a cacophony of noise and chaos.

Of course—Tammuz would be delighted with this anarchy.

"What's different between me and Mortana? Unlike her, I'm loyal." I turned, grabbed the flaming chair, and hurled it at him. He blocked it, but his dark clothes caught fire. Flames rose around him, gilding his features. He patted out the flames, trying to salvage what was left of his clothes.

"You're loyal? Doesn't look that way to me." His shirt had burned almost completely away, leaving black rags draped over his thickly muscled chest.

Another distraction Tammuz hadn't prepared me for.

"Not loyal to you," I said. "You've been telling me quite consistently how much you hate me. No, sorry. You don't respect me enough to hate me because I'm *boring* and talentless. Why would you expect me to be loyal to you?"

My temper soared.

I was done being pushed around, and I didn't have to take it anymore. I lunged at him, punching him hard in the jaw with a loud crack of bone. The force of the blow dazed him for a moment, and I kicked him the chest. He slammed back into a hot stone wall, and it cracked behind him. Before he could recover, I shifted, aiming my next kick at his head, but his hand shot out and he grabbed my right ankle with shocking speed.

His dark eyes glinted, and the mark of Lucifer shone from his head. Was it just me, or was he enjoying himself a little, holding my ankle in his steely grip at his shoulder?

I let my wings burst open, lifting me into the air, and slammed my other foot into his head. His skull shot back into the wall, but as I retracted my wings and landed, he charged me, knocking me flat on my back. He moved to leap on top of me, but I lifted my legs, trapping his throat between my thighs. I squeezed hard, but he lifted me up from under my ass.

Spinning around, he slammed me down again on the burning bed. Fire engulfed us. I didn't feel a thing apart from Orion's waist between my thighs.

He tried to pin me down by the wrists, but before he got a good grip, I smashed my left elbow into his temple, then smacked him on the other side with my right, knocking him off me and onto the burning floor.

I landed on top of him, straddling his waist. Now was the time to act. I drew out my claws—

He trapped my wrists, and we strained against each other, his fierce, shadowy gaze locked on mine. "Am I about to die, just as I started to live again?" he asked.

I had no idea what that meant. Getting in my head again.

And what would happen if I got my hands free? Could I really end Orion's life?

I was pretty sure he could have ended mine on the bed if he'd simply swiped for my heart instead of grabbing me by the wrists.

That gave me pause.

Sweat rolled down my temples.

I brought my forehead down, breaking his nose. He dropped my wrists, and I brought out my long silver claws.

I slashed for him.

CHAPTER 33—ROWAN

 hen it came down to it, I couldn't kill Orion, so I settled for slashing his throat with my claws instead. His blood pumped over the black and white mosaic, and I leapt off him. I didn't know how long it would take for him to recover, but I wasn't going to wait around to find out.

With a pounding heart, I crossed over to the unconscious king. The smoke from the fires had started to fill my lungs and sting my eyes. Coughing, I bent down and scooped up Cambriel. The knife still jutted from his heart, and his mouth gaped open, blood streaking down his chest.

Holding his limp body in my arms, I ran out on the balcony, blinking in the bright morning sun. In the sweet, fresh air, I inhaled deeply, clearing my eyes of smoke and sweat.

My wings shot out of my shoulders, and the wind

rushed over them. Beneath me, the army swarmed, tiny as ants.

I flew off the balcony and into the honey-rose sky, soaring above the dawn-kissed demon city. Beneath me, soldiers were scrambling, still bound by their oaths to protect their living king. But soon, they would pledge their loyalty to me. I wanted them to see what was about to happen to their false king, the charlatan on the throne.

I *really* wanted to kill him in front of my parents' house. Poetic, but not the best strategy. It was too far, and I'd have to wait for the army to catch up. I wasn't going to waste another moment.

I streaked toward the sandy stones of the Luciferian ward, not far from the tower, unleashing a stream of fire as I raced toward the earth. Total chaos ensued, disrupting the arrows that might come for me. As I drew closer, I cleared a space on the amber stones with tongues of fire.

I landed hard on the stones but managed to steady myself. The Acheron River flowed behind me. In real time, it wasn't that long ago that I'd been sitting at a nearby restaurant eating pasta, convinced I was mortal. Not long ago, I'd passed the initiation in the wilderness, using fox piss, deodorant, and lighters to save my own life.

Firmly on solid earth once more, I looked up to see the demon army charging me, stones rumbling at the horde's approach. I had to protect myself before they ripped me to pieces.

I surrounded the prostrate king and myself with a

circle of flames, watching the army halt on the other side. This was it. I didn't have long.

"Only the true heir can slaughter a king," I shouted. "I am here to prove to you that I am your queen."

Silence reigned. The hairs on the back of my neck stood up, a sixth sense that danger lurked behind me. Lifting my gaze, I saw Orion hurtling through the sky, wings outstretched, headed straight for me. I dropped the king and rose to meet him. We collided in midair, wings thrashing, and grappled with one another. He grabbed me by the waist and tossed me aside, and I veered clumsily toward the earth, arms wheeling.

I righted myself again, and horror unfurled beneath me. Orion was on top of the king. Landing on his back, I tried to pull him off, but it was over in an instant.

Orion ripped the king's chest open, clawing out his heart in a single stroke. He lifted it into the air, brandishing it above his head. Seething with bitter disappointment, I saw the five-pointed star beaming from his head.

I'd done that. I'd figured out how to kill the king. How to get past his army. How to kill him in public. And Orion had swept in at the last moment to steal my victory. I shook with anger.

I wanted to shout that it was mine, that Orion had stolen the king's heart from me. This was *my* revenge. Cambriel had killed *my* mom, not his. Orion had taken that from me, and the crown with it, but there was no way to say it without sounding petulant and insane. But it wasn't just about me, was it? Orion was going to fucking murder everyone.

The flames were dying down around us, and the army of soldiers in midnight blue knelt for their new king. Red-hot jealousy burned through me.

Yes, I wanted power. Who didn't? When you had power, you could stop the crazy people from burning the world down.

The placid smile on Orion's beautiful face sent molten rage through my veins.

He lifted the king's heart again, blood dripping down his arm. The rising sun washed him in gold—a beautiful god of wrath. "Cambriel was not your true king. It was I who slaughtered Nergal, and *I* who will right the wrongs of your former kings. No longer will we live in a jail of mortal making. No longer will I allow them to control us. Together, we will find a way to break the bonds that trap us here and once again become gods!"

The crowd roared, and ice slid through my veins. They were eating this up.

Orion turned to look at me, his expression glacial, and I gritted my teeth.

"Escort this woman out of my realm," he boomed. "She tried to burn down the Tower of Baal. She is not allowed within our city walls."

"What are you doing?" I demanded.

"What I promised from the beginning. I told you that I would banish you from the city. I can't be around you, Rowan."

I glanced at the soldiers marching for me, then back to him. "The mortal police will arrest me. Immediately."

His eyes danced with cold amusement. "You're resourceful. I can see that now. I'm sure you'll think of something."

The crowd was shouting his name, ecstatic. Bare-chested, Orion glowed with amber light, looking every bit a king. I inhaled deeply, breathing in the scent of smoke and blood. Red sun rays beamed down on us through soot and cinders.

If the Lord of Chaos succeeds, the mortal realm will burn.

My gaze flicked to the oncoming soldiers, and I wanted to scream.

Why wait to be escorted out? Unfurling my wings, I rose into the ashen sky.

I would see myself out—but I'd be back.

Of that, I had no doubt.

CHAPTER 34—ROWAN

From Shai's hotel room at the top of the Glover Inn, I had a perfect view of the historic district of Osborne. The climates were different in the underworld and the City of Thorns, and it was strange to see that it was still autumn here, the trees bursting with fiery colors under the glow of the streetlights.

This was the nice part of Wallcott Street, with colorfully painted shops, brick sidewalks, and gold signs. Warmth shone from the windows of brick buildings, and people walked around with steaming cups of coffee and hot chocolate. A narrow, cobbled road sloped down toward shadowy Witchcraft Point. Even that looked nice from here—orange dots in the darkness.

How was Mr. Esposito doing tonight? I would absolutely have checked on him if it didn't involved returning to the scene of a crime.

And from here, I could see all the way up the opposite

hill. In the distance, the City of Thorns glowed with pale light the color of butter. I pressed my palms against the glass, fogging the window a little.

How long before Orion arrived and started killing people?

The door opened, and I turned to see Shai wearing a black turtleneck and a short tweed skirt. She was carrying two wine glasses. "I got these from the bar downstairs. Cheaper than room service."

I sighed, taking in the cozy hotel room. Walnut book-shelves lined the walls on either side of the fireplace. Shai slid the wine glasses onto a desk by the window. "They're both for you."

"You're not having any?"

"I got permission to go back into the City of Thorns. I don't think Orion trusts me because of my connection to you, but the oath he made to me included a promise to keep me safe. He can't really keep me safe if I'm not in the kingdom, can he?"

I let out a long sigh. "Why wasn't I clever enough to demand an oath like that?"

"I was raised by two parents who were constantly learning how to one-up each other. It's an art form." She crossed to the wardrobe and pulled it open. "You should stay here for a while, though. I can pay for it. Isn't this room amazing?"

My gaze wandered around the space. In a weird way, it reminded me of the coziness of the underworld cabin —lots of dark wood and candles for ambiance. Except here, there was unmistakable luxury: a red velvet comforter, bookshelves crammed with beautiful old volumes, and an antique mahogany desk by the window.

Rain started to fall against the glass.

In her elegant skirt and black sweater, Shai looked like she belonged here.

"Thank you, Shai. It's beautiful. But I'm not sure it's a great idea to stay in a room with your name or credit card info. Jack and the mortal police have already connected us." I sighed. "It's only a matter of time before they find me here."

She pulled out her suitcase. "Okay. Where will you go, then?"

"Into hiding, I guess." I didn't really have a plan yet, but I knew I could live through winter with almost nothing. "I'll forage for acorns and berries in a forest."

She pulled on her wool coat. "I'm serious. Why can't you try to convince Orion to at least let you back in the city?"

"Because I'm his rival, and even if I weren't, he doesn't like me." Oddly, after everything I'd been through, the words stung worse than an arrow through my ribs.

"You can't charm him?"

I handed her one of the glasses of wine. "You're going to want a sip of this, Shai. Sit down for a second."

In her coat, she perched on the end of the bed and took a sip of wine. "Okay. You're scaring me. What's happening?"

I twirled my wineglass. "I haven't been sure how to tell you this, but Orion is going to kill everyone."

Her brown eyes widened. "Sorry, what?"

"Not in the City of Thorns, although I'm sure he'll kill a fair number there, too. But mostly out here. He wants to murder all the mortals. He thinks he can find a way to break the spell that keeps demons bound to the city, and he wants to set them free. To feed. To get revenge."

Her mouth opened and closed. "I always knew he was unhinged. Is that really possible, though?"

"Orion will probably find a way to do it. This is a man who dug himself out of a dungeon over a century, and the whole time, he was dreaming of murdering mortals. For all his other flaws, he gets shit done in the most impossible circumstances. And he's all fucked up."

She tilted her head back and drained her glass. When she'd finished, she wiped her mouth. "Okay. We need to tell everyone. We need to *evacuate* everyone."

"To where? He's not going to stop at Osborne."

She set the empty wine glass on the desk. "Please tell me you have an idea of what to do. What about that forest god?"

I took a deep breath. "I've been thinking of going to see him, but I don't get the sense he cares if mortals die. He's actually really into death. I think he helped me because he wanted to make the fight for the throne a little more interesting."

"But it's over, right?" she asked. "Orion is king now. There's no changing that."

A lump rose in my throat, and I swallowed hard. "If I want to stop him, I'll have to kill him."

"You? You can't kill him!" She stared at me. "I'm sorry, Rowan, I'm having a hard time adjusting to your killer demon abilities. I still think of you as the person who got nervous and puked at graduation."

"Yeah, me, too." I watched the rain pelt the glass. "Look, Shai, you should go to the City of Thorns. We know it's safe there. And I'm going to figure something out. I'll come up with a plan, I promise. I'll stay here a little longer to clear my head."

Her phone buzzed, and she pulled it out of her pocket. "Shit. My Uber is here."

"Go. We'll be in touch over text."

Her gaze flicked to the window. "What are you going to do if the police show up?"

"At the rate my magic is draining, I should be able to fly for a few more days. I'll be fine. And after that, they'll never find me." Insanely, I was even considering hiding out in the underworld cabin.

She hurried toward the door. "Okay. Text me, if you can. I'm leaving you the hotel keys. You can stay here for a week if you don't think you'll get caught."

When she shut the door, I dimmed the lights a little, preferring the candlelight. I sipped the wine and stared out the window. I'd failed, yes. But that couldn't be it. My parents had given their lives trying to keep me safe, believing Orion must not rule. I couldn't bear to think of how disappointed they'd be right now, knowing that he'd won. My chest ached.

A clanking sound made my ears perk up.

I looked to the right and caught a glimpse of someone shuffling along the sidewalk on a walker. It was Mr. Esposito, getting drenched in the rain. Why was he always out in this weather? He really needed looking after.

As he walked past the hotel, I saw him drop something—a brown paper bag.

Damn it. It was lying there in a puddle now, and he hadn't even realized. I tapped the window a few times, trying to get his attention, but he shambled on down the hill.

I grabbed a key, left the room, and hurried down all four flights of creaking stairs. Rushing past the receptionist, I went out the front door.

Mr. Esposito was gone. The hotel sat on the peak of the hill. Streetlights gleamed off puddles, and rivulets of rain streamed down the deserted cobbled streets. Everyone had scrambled inside to get away from the storm.

The old man had vanished. I wasn't sure how he'd been able to move that quickly, but maybe he'd taken cover indoors, too.

His little brown paper bag still lay on the sidewalk in the rain. I jogged over and snatched it off the ground, planning to drop it by his house later. Tucking it under my arm, I pushed the buzzer to get back into the hotel.

What was in the bag—a book, maybe? While I waited for the receptionist, I turned the sack over and found the letter *R* written on it.

R for Rowan?

Curiosity sparked, and I opened the bag and peered inside. It *was* a book, one that looked far too old and precious to be left in a puddle. But someone had carefully wrapped it in plastic to protect it. A velvety midnight blue cover was embossed with gold text, filigrees, and little symbols of stars. The title jumped out at me.

Trial by Combat in the Demon World.

I stared at the book, my mind ticking back to something Mr. Esposito had said the night I'd killed the congressman: "Get to the City of Thorns."

He knew, didn't he?

What if there were more...

Cambriel had feared that if he let my parents in the city, he'd have to allow more Lilu entry. Maybe he'd known something.

I was so stunned that I nearly missed the buzz of the door. Pushing inside, I ran up the stairs and back into Shai's room. I hurried to the desk, then sat down and carefully pulled the book from the plastic.

As I cracked it open, my pulse raced. This felt like a message to me. Long ago, King Nergal had taken the crown from my grandfather Azriel in trial by combat.

I sipped the wine Shai had left for me and started to read. As the rain pattered against the window, I learned more about the demonic beliefs concerning monarchy. Demons believe that when a crown is contested, the gods will choose the winner. A series of trials determines who is suited to rule. When a demon with a legitimate claim wants to challenge a ruler, they make a public declaration.

I looked up from the book, gazing but unseeing, into the darkness outside the window.

This was what Tammuz had prepared me for.

I was going back to the City of Thorns.

* * *

YOU CAN PREORDER the third book in the series—Garden of Serpents. In book three, you will be reading about **redemption**.

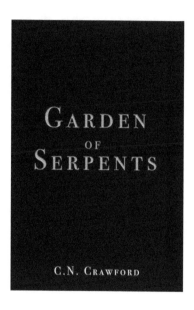

Join me and other readers in discussions about this book, and what to read next, in C.N. Crawford's Coven.

ALSO BY C.N. CRAWFORD

For a full list of our books, please check out our website, cncrawford.com. You can find a free book there.

Amazon and goodreads also have a full listing of our books. Reviews are appreciated!

Read on for a sample of a completed series—the Shadow Fae series—to see if that is what you want to read next!

COURT OF SHADOWS—SAMPLE CHAPTER

The vampire bared his fangs, and I knew we'd both be dead by the end of the night if I didn't get him out of here. I leapt over the bar with the speed of a hurricane wind, hurtling toward him. I slammed my fist into his skull—once, twice, three times. He staggered back, then collapsed. He'd fallen so easily I almost didn't feel a sense of victory, but I grinned down at him anyway. The colored lights of the bar stained his porcelain skin red.

I *had* to get him out of here.

I tried to project a calm I didn't feel. "Like I said," I purred, "a guy like you would be more comfortable in a hipster joint with arcade games and herbal cocktails. You can talk about synthwave or whatever there. Move along. *Now.*" I may have screamed the last word. A sense of urgency was taking over.

It was at that point, I realized that everyone in the bar had stopped talking and were all staring at me over their pints. A pop song crackled through the speakers, and the neon sign in the window flickered on and off. Otherwise, silence shrouded us.

Easy, Arianna. Easy. I stood over the fallen vampire, holding up my hands. "Nothing to see here, folks! Just an ordinary Friday night kerfuffle."

I loosed a long sigh. Two thin hawthorn stakes jutted from my messy bun, ready for the vampire's heart, but I restrained myself. My boss would flip his shit if he saw me beating up customers—again. And I definitely wasn't supposed to kill people—even if they were undead—in front of a crowd. Rufus frowned upon things like that in his establishment.

You can take the girl out of the gladiator arena....

It was just unfortunate that the vampire had made the serious error of trying to bite me.

As soon as this guy had stumbled into our bar, I'd known he was trouble. In fact, I'd immediately assessed three important things about him.

One, his luxurious Viking beard had told me he was a hipster—not to mention his neon clothing, reminiscent of children's wear in the early 1980s. Whenever guys dressed like him decided to slum it in the Spread Eagle, it usually went down badly with the regulars.

Two, his staggering gait and furrowed brow had told me that he was a mean, sloppy drunk. Given the exceptional alcohol tolerance levels of vampires, he must have drunk his weight in craft beers tonight.

Three, and worst of all, he was a supernatural.

I cocked my head at him as he lay on the floor. He *might* even be old enough that the medieval Norseman beard was actually authentic. Supernaturals like him— like me—were outlawed these days. We had to fly under the radar if we wanted to live. Too bad this one was too stupid to keep a low profile. Four years of executions and assassinations, and this fucker had just brazenly walked into our bar, flashing his fangs around.

As the patrons turned back to their pint glasses, pretending to ignore us, I frowned at the hipster-vampire. Dazed, he still lay on the beer-stained floor, but he'd managed to push himself up onto his elbows. The undead bastards didn't stay down for long. His pale eyes were trained on me, possibly recognizing my own magic.

Ciara, my oldest friend, crept over to us, her brown eyes wide. Her hand was clamped over her grin. I could tell she was stopping just short of clapping her hands. "Oh my goodness, Arianna. You punched him. Do you see his fangs?" She had a sweet but unfortunate tendency to idolize supernaturals, like we were some kind of celebrities. After all, there weren't many of us around these days. "A real, live vampire," she whispered, pointing at him.

"I can hear you," the vamp slurred, now rising to his feet. He staggered closer. "Little girl."

"I need to get him out of here," I muttered. And I had to do it without using any of my magic. You never knew who was watching, ready to turn you in.

Now, my new Viking friend's gaze was locked on

Ciara. Red flashed in his eyes. He was after blood tonight, and she was clearly an easier target than me. It didn't help that she was wearing a T-shirt featuring a male model with fangs poking from pouty lips. She gods-damned loved vampires.

"I know your game, little girl." The vampire licked his fangs, swaying on his feet. "You read your little books about teenagers falling in love with thousand-year-old vamps. Our skin is supposed to sparkle like a unicorn's arse, right? And you all get a happy ending. Wrong. Those books are crap. Come with me, and I'll teach you about reading real literature. Hemingway, Kerouac, Bukowski—"

His monologue was cut off by the sight of the thin stake I'd pulled out of my hair. I twirled it between my fingers, and the vampire seemed hypnotized by the movement.

I smiled at him. "Now that you're quiet, let's get one thing straight. I will not have you slandering romance books in my bar." Technically, it wasn't my bar, but that was beside the point. This arsehole thought he was going to feed on Ciara. And moreover, I would not tolerate anyone banging on about Bukowski. "I'd like to just get back to the shots of Johnny Walker I was drinking before you came in, and I don't want to have to keep punching you. I'd prefer not to get your blood on my new miniskirt. So run along. I'm pretty sure an ironic meth-trailer-themed bar just opened up a few blocks away." I leaned closer, arching an eyebrow. "It seems more your scene."

Despite the arse-kicking I'd just given him and the stake in my hand, he seemed unfazed.

He stumbled toward Ciara. "I think I'd be more comfortable if your friend came with me."

I gave him a hard shove, and he staggered back.

The door swung open, and a second vamp came in— this one in a visor, a handlebar mustache, and a pink bow tie. Had someone told them we had a sale on ukuleles or something?

I had to get them out of here. The last thing I wanted was for the Spread Eagle to attract the spell-slayers' attention for harboring supernaturals.

I flashed the two vamps a dark smile. "No supernaturals allowed in here. No supernaturals allowed *anywhere*. Those are the rules. You've got ten seconds to leave this bar," I said sweetly, while calculating all the ways I could kill them. "Or I might start getting angry. And you don't want that to happen."

Viking Vamp snorted, then his irises flared with red. The air seemed to thin around us. "And what the fuck are you, pretty thing? You're not human."

My blood chilled. I couldn't let anyone overhear him saying that.

He snatched a whisky bottle—my whisky bottle— from the bar, his movements lightning fast. Then, he jabbed a finger in my face. "You're not supposed to be here, either. I think I just might tell the spell-slayers on you. Tick tock. Your time is running out, pretty lady. But give me a look at those gorgeous tits of yours and I might keep your secret."

Rage surged. And then, as I registered the word "spell-slayers," dread slithered up my spine.

Okay. I was done being nice. Now he had to die.

There was only one thing in London scarier than me, and that was the spell-slayers. The fae assassins haunted London's streets in dark cloaks, blending into the night sky like smoke. They terrorized humans and magical creatures alike, ruling the city with the points of their blades, silently slaughtering in the shadows. No one was supposed to look them in the eye, or speak to them, or breathe in their direction. But we all owed them a tithe from our paychecks. Protection money, they called it. They were no better than a magical mafia. In short, they were the worst. I hated them and feared them in equal measure.

I narrowed my eyes at the vamps. "You want me to believe you're brave enough to attract the attention of the spell-slayers? And risk your own necks? Bollocks. You're supposed to be locked up in a magical realm with all the other supernaturals, not roaming London's streets. I'm now four seconds away from dragging you outside and staking you."

Truth was, I'd stake them whether or not they left willingly. I couldn't risk them turning me in.

I didn't really have time for too many mental calculations, because the next thing I knew, Viking Vamp was lunging for Ciara again, fangs bared.

Fast—maybe faster than I should have—I pivoted around him, pointing my stake at his neck. I wasn't supposed to move too quickly; humans were slow and sluggish. But the sight of him attacking Ciara sent my blood racing, and instinct kicked in.

I pressed the stake against his jugular. Then, I stood on my tiptoes, whispering into his ear. "I know a stake to the neck won't kill you. But I will make it hurt when I jam it into your throat and wiggle it round. Then I'll kill you."

Something sharp jabbed into my back, stopping me in my tracks. A quick glance over my shoulder told me that his friend, Visor Vamp, was holding a knife to my back.

"Drop the stake, darling!" said Visor Vamp.

Baleros's third law of power: Always let your enemy underestimate you.

I dropped the stake. I held up my hands as if I were surrendering, adding in a bit of trembling for good measure.

Then, when I felt the point of the knife retreat a little, I pivoted, slamming my elbow into his nose. I brought up my knee into his crotch—three brutal cracks to the groin. Vamps might not be alive, but they were still sensitive in the usual places. As he bent forward, I twisted his arm, forcing him to the ground. I snatched the knife from his hand at the same time. Then, I pointed it at his neck.

My lips curled in a mocking smile. "You still want to play?"

Now, at last, the vamps had the good sense to look scared. Apart from a warbling pop song, the room had gone silent again.

Viking Vamp held up his hands. "We'll leave."

I pulled the blade away from the other's neck. As he straightened, he leaned in close, breathing in my ear. "The spell-slayers will be coming for you."

At that, an icy tendril of dread coiled through my chest.

I watched as the two vamps skulked out of the bar.

I jammed my hand into the pocket of my miniskirt, and I pulled out a lollipop. Cherry, with gum in the center. Nothing like crystalized sugar to calm the nerves. I popped it in my mouth, staring at the door.

Ciara grinned. "Well geez Louise, this has been a heck of an evening." She'd lived in the UK for at least ten years now and still hadn't lost her thick American accent. "I haven't been this excited since my Aunt Starlene drew a clown on my bedroom wall to ease my loneliness."

"It's not over." There'd been something too cocky about those vamps, and their parting shot had told me everything I needed to know. I'd heard of some supernaturals acting as informants to the spell-slayers. Supernatural narcs. Maybe that was how these two idiots had managed to stay alive, biting humans like Ciara with impunity. "Can you cover the bar while I'm out?"

"No problem."

I had a pair of vampires to kill.

* * *

I snatched my stake off the floor, then my backpack. I never went anywhere without it. My bug-out bag had everything I might need in an emergency: a headlamp, a lighter with aerosolized deodorant for smelling nice or lighting things on fire, medical supplies, a water bottle, cherry lip gloss, fresh knickers, a shortwave radio, ropes, assorted lollipops, duct tape, and a shitload of knives. Never say I wasn't prepared.

The door creaked as I pushed through it into the night air. A sooty bridge arched over the Spread Eagle, where pigeons made their home in the shadows. They cooed above me.

I tossed my lollipop in a rubbish bin. I didn't like to kill things with sweets in my mouth.

Shivering a little in the misty air, I scanned the dark streets under the bridge until I saw movement. The two vamps were moving toward the Tower—the seat of spell-slayer power. I wouldn't let them get any closer to its walls.

I trailed behind them over the damp, cobbled road, moving silently. A light rain misted over my skin, curling my lavender hair.

Quickening my pace, I drew the hawthorn stakes from my hair, holding one in each hand like a pair of daggers. My pulse raced, heart quickening with the thrill of the hunt. I had them in my sights, and I wasn't letting them get anywhere.

When I'd come up behind them, I crooned, "Hey, vamps."

They whirled, and I slammed my stakes into their hearts. And just like that, the fight was over.

Baleros's sixth law of power: Crush your enemies mercilessly.

Their eyes went wide, but within seconds, they had crumbled to piles of ash on the pavement. Rain dampened their blackened remains.

I pulled my stakes from the ash and wiped them off with a tissue from my bag. As I did, I lifted my eyes to the medieval fortress before me. Once, it had simply been known as the Tower of London. Now, people called it the Institute. It was the one place the spell-slayers hadn't outlawed magic. Even from here, I could see its walls and towers brimming with sorcery. Pale blue light streamed from the stony spires into the skies, and a moat of golden light surrounded the entire structure.

The spell-slayers claimed they'd outlawed magic to keep the peace. They said that the apocalyptic wars twenty years ago—the ones between angels, fae, and demons—were forever at risk of erupting again. They said all supernaturals should remain segregated and locked in magical realms. Apparently, only the fae nobility were capable and worthy of remaining neutral among the human world. Everyone else was an animal, you see.

But I knew how the spell-slayers really thought. Magic was power, and they wanted it all for themselves. I hated them with an intensity that rivaled the brilliance of their gleaming spires.

I turned, walking back to the Spread Eagle. As I did, I tucked the hawthorn stakes back into my hair. I'd rid myself of that threat quickly enough. So why did I still feel that eerie sense of dread hanging over me?

When I slipped back into the bar, I found that another grim hush had overtaken the place, and my heart started to race.

I scanned the room until I figured out why.

When my gaze landed on a fae male in the corner, my blood began roaring in my ears.

I glimpsed a sweep of black hair under his cowl. The neon lights of the bar flashed over olive skin and vibrant green eyes. His broad shoulders took up half the booth, and an opening in his cloak revealed leather armor underneath. I had no doubt that every inch of his body was muscled and strapped with weapons. He held himself with a preternatural stillness, gazing at me like a snake about to strike. My stomach dropped.

Fae nobility, and a spell-slayer. Like so many of his kind, he was shockingly beautiful and terrifying at the same time. Under his stare, I felt uncharacteristically self-conscious in my bargain-basement miniskirt that was just a little too short. Of course, spell-slayers like him wanted everyone else to feel like crap. They lived to dominate and terrify. They'd mastered messing with people's heads.

And right now, I was certain he'd come for me, even if I'd tried to be careful.

If I turned and ran now, it would confirm my guilt, and he'd be after me instantly.

My gaze slid to the bar, where Ciara was trying to act

natural, although her hands were shaking as she pulled a pint.

Rufus, our boss, now stood by her side. The presence of the spell-slayers had unnerved him, too, and I could see sweat droplets beading at the edges of his graying hair. Ciara and Rufus weren't even supernaturals, and the slayer still scared the crap out of them.

Rufus met my gaze, his eyes flicking wide open. The strained look on his face said, *Get the hell over here. Now.*

Swallowing hard, I crossed to him. I watched as he pulled our most expensive bottle of wine—which, let's be honest, was something he'd picked up from Tesco, simply labeled *French Red Wine.* Staring across the bar at the spell-slayer, he poured a glass.

I cast a quick glance at myself in the mirror behind Rufus. Straight eyebrows, high cheekbones, amber eyes. The only thing that might have marked me as a supernatural was the pale lavender shade of my hair, but plenty of humans dyed their hair bright colors these days. My fae canines and pointed ears only emerged when I thought my life was in danger, which didn't happen often. In other words, I could pass for human. Maybe he'd come for the vampires, instead?

"Take these over to him," whispered Rufus. "Tell him it's our best wine. Tell him it's on the house. Tell him we'll give him money. Tell him—" His eyes suddenly narrowed. "You didn't happen to see anything unusual tonight, did you?" He was still pouring the wine, and it spilled over the rim, pooling on the bar like blood.

I loosed a long sigh. I often found Rufus staring at the

blank walls in his office, listlessly licking his yogurt spoon over and over. I honestly had no idea how someone like him had survived the apocalypse at all.

"Nothing unusual." I gently took the bottle from his hand. Might as well not give the guy a complete heart attack.

"Don't look him in the eyes," Rufus hissed, his eyes wide.

My gaze flicked back to the spell-slayer, and my stomach leapt as I realized his eyes were still on me. My throat went dry. There was no way in hell I was bringing him wine.

I was quickly realizing there was no way out of this situation without fighting a spell-slayer. And I knew only too well how vicious they could be.

"Actually, Rufus … I'm not feeling so well."

"You what?" He sounded incredulous.

"Lady stuff."

"Oh." He fell silent. Apparently, that topic was more terrifying than the spell slayer.

"Gotta run. I'll see you tomorrow." I cast a quick glance at Ciara as I headed for the door. She was the only one around who knew I was a demi-fae. Baleros—my former gladiator master—had once assigned her to tend to my wounds between matches in the arena. Ciara and I had slept in the same cage for years. She knew my dreams and my nightmares. She knew why the scent of roses made me sick. She knew almost everything about me.

Almost.

As soon as I'd slipped outside into the damp air, I shoved my hand into my bug-out bag, rummaging around until I found my iron knife, sheathed in leather. I hated having to use iron. It was poisonous to fae like me, but it was the only way to hurt a spell-slayer.

Then, I pulled out my mobile and called Ciara.

"Arianna," she answered immediately, whispering into the phone. "He's still here. And now there's another one, with violet eyes. I've heard of him. He's the one they call the Wraith. He moves like wind in the night and slaughters silently in the shadows. I think he's the Devil himself."

"Very reassuring, thanks." She was always saying weird shit about the Devil. Pretty sure it was an American thing. Whatever the case, this was not wonderful news. "Just tell me when they're leaving."

"The Devil wears many faces," she hissed.

"I know. Just simmer down, friend. Look, I might have to fight them both. Just text me when they leave."

"Wait. Wait. If you make it home alive, put cat pee in front of your door, mixed with old cabbage."

"Is that supposed to ward off fae nobility?"

"Dunno, but Aunt Starlene put it outside our trailer to keep the police away after she threw an alligator at someone in a McDonald's parking lot. And she set bear traps." She scratched her cheek. "Also, she might have shot them, so … that could have actually been the part that kept them out of our trailer."

"Thanks, Ciara. Gotta go." I shoved my mobile back in my pocket.

Dread bloomed in my chest.

Baleros's ninth law of power: Don't attack unless you're certain you can win.

I'd been trained by a spell-slayer. I knew how they fought.

As a gladiator, I'd often fought multiple opponents at once, taking them out within minutes. I had been the only female gladiator, and my stage name had been the Amazon Terror. The amount of blood I'd spilled had been more than enough to appease the crowds, and Baleros, because he was a complete prick, had fashioned special armor that emphasized my boobs. I'd been quite the attraction.

But spell-slayers were different than anyone I'd fought in the arena. They were ancient, disciplined, with centuries of exquisite training far beyond my own. My chances of winning in a fight against two of them were a little lower than my chances of sprouting wings and flying off to freedom. Before I flung my knife at them, I'd wait to see if they attacked first.

My phone buzzed, and I pulled it out to read the text.

They're leaving.

Adrenaline raced through my blood, and I dodged into an alleyway. It's not like I could really hide, though. Fae trackers like them would be able to smell me.

I quickened my pace, but I'd only gone a few steps before the hairs on the back of my neck stood on end. I could feel them watching me, and my pulse started racing out of control. A cold sweat dampened my brow.

How had they gotten here so fast?

I gripped the hilt of the knife hard, and I whirled.

A pit opened in my stomach at the sight of two cloaked spell-slayers standing just behind me. Frigid panic rippled up my spine.

* * *

To read more of this completed series, check out Shadow Fae on Amazon.

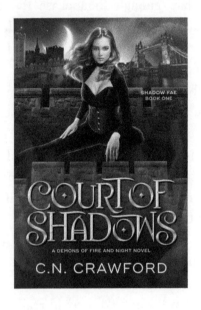

ACKNOWLEDGMENTS

Thanks to Michael Omer for his help making my characters come alive, and for helping me to think about logic—not my strong suit.

Thanks to Lauren Ann, my assistant for helping me publicize the book.

Lauren and Jean are my fabulous editors for this book.

Thanks to my advanced reader team for their help in making it truly shine, and to C.N. Crawford's Coven!